A

CANDLELIGHT GEORGIAN SPECIAL

Turning toward the large, foster_critique_of

Candlelight Regencies

The Education of Joanne

by
Joan Vincent

A CANDLELIGHT GEORGIAN SPECIAL

Published by
Dell Publishing Co., Inc.
1 Dag Hammarskjold Plaza
New York, New York 10017

Dell ® TM 681510, Dell Publishing Co., Inc.

ISBN: 0-440-12303-8

Printed in the United States of America

First printing—July 1980

To all those whose help turned
a pessimist into an optimist

...got out there's keen sight as she tucked a fresh sheet over her. "Quickly, girls, clear the chamber.

The Education
of Joanne

Chapter One

"It shall not be tolerated!" roared the Earl of Furness, his pallid, powdered complexion highlighted by dulled patches of anger. "This time she has outdone the extremes of folly! Was a father ever more cursed with such a vexatious child?" he asked, turning to Lady Evelyn.

In answer to his question his timid sister ventured no answer despite the multitude of words rioting to break the barricade of her lips, for she was accustomed to her brother's outbursts in regard to his only daughter. Instead she chose to inspect the puffs of her polonaise gown.

"What can be done with her? What action have I not tried?" Lord Furness continued, his ire growing. "I shall seal her in her chambers for this. She shall not flaunt . . ."

"Dear brother," Lady Evelyn interrupted, "calm yourself before you bring on apoplexy. Surely Joanne's behaviour cannot . . ."

"Cannot! Exactly," he thundered, waving the missive in his hand, his lace cuff brushing her face. "She has undone all my effort—none in the realm but riff-raff and scum will have her after this is known. Even they will succumb only if the temptation is generous enough."

His port-laden breath assured Lady Evelyn that her brother's ravings were just a continuation of the usual tone regarding his daughter.

"Have you nothing to say? You could have aided me with this child," he baited as he meticulously arranged the ruffles of his shirt front.

"I was repulsed in my offer to do so," she said, rising angrily, her ire roused at this unjust charge. "I told you I would raise the child as my own—see to her education—but you protested. Now live with the results of *your* education of Joanne." The words were regretted as soon as they were sounded—not for any element of untruth, but for the effect they would have on her brother.

"Damn the whole bloody business," said Lord Furness in a much milder tone than Lady Evelyn had braced herself for. The touch of despair in the tone drew her eyes to his face. Troubled, pained, his eyes burned into her own and she was lost for words of comfort, consolation, or confident solution. The eyes, she thought, how like the daughter's to the father's—would either ever be free of anguish?

Lord, that I might help them both, she thought. The prayer was instantly crushed by her acknowledgment of habitual submission to her brother. The time for correcting the wrong had long since passed. She had not been able to withstand his decision to isolate his infant daughter upon the death of the mother. Nor had she been able to take hold when she had visited Furness House and seen the child, then only seven years of age and already filled with a growing bile; at so young an age, the child was already tormented by the realization that her life was begrudged by her father. There was no way Lady Evelyn could help and her timid soul shrank from the remembrance of the child's unharnessed hostility. How this hostility must have grown in the three and ten years of continued neglect!

Lost in these thoughts, Lady Evelyn had not followed her brother's mumblings. ". . . education lacked nothing. The best governess to be had—why you even recommended some that were used over the years." He strode to the slab table at the side of the small sitting room and poured a glass of port. Downing it, he refilled and emptied the glass once again. Furness mused in gentler tones as he turned back to Lady Evelyn, "If only Joanna had not died . . ." The gentleness, peculiar to any thought of his wife, flitted across his features momentarily, altering forcibly as he ended bitterly, "Or at least if it was a son who had caused her death."

Lady Evelyn sighed hopelessly. Her brother had never reconciled himself to his wife's death; she had survived the childbed only six months, her frailty tested too far by the difficult birth.

"What is it she has done?" she asked, absently wondering the cause of his verbal violence this time.

Anger creased his face. "She has poured a vase of putrid flowers on the Viscount of Fordingham and told him he was lucky she did not crack his skull with

it—this after he had offered for her hand in marriage."
Lord Furness spoke in the tone of a magistrate citing
a death-warranted offense.

"Fordingham—Blayworth's son? That spindly, bald-
ing fop? There is no wonder—I dare not comprehend
how he had the courage to approach Joanne. They
say he will not even put a hand to the reins," Lady
Evelyn noted, suspicion entering her voice at the end.
"How . . ."

"Well you are to wonder how. For months I have
been plying that sniveling coward—enduring his
presence and worse, his discourses. What is the reward
for my labours?"

"This," he again waved the missive, "is from Fordingham withdrawing his offer. I should never have
permitted him to see her until the day they were to
wed. Now, if all the land and wealth I have will not in-
duce *him* to tolerate marriage with her, not even one
of convenience, who am I to find?"

"Why, I had no idea you intended her to marry.
You have never even brought the child to London,
never given her a ball—never let her go beyond the
grounds of Furness. Your behaviour regarding the
child has not prepared her for . . . But, why not find a
genteel woman to educate Joanne in the finer arts of
society—to prepare her for a London season? Next
spring would be the time—shortly before she is to be
one and twenty. A bit old, I must say so myself," she
said, fanning herself with her bejeweled, painted fan,
"but some rumour can be put about—ill-health mayhap. This woman could teach Joanne the manners of
the *beau monde* since you feel she is lacking in the
more gentle womanly qualities. Refine her and teach

her how to dress. I . . . I would be willing to sponsor her," she offered with false gaiety, her tall periwig of massive curls swaying as she spoke.

"When did you last see the child—ten, four and ten years past? You would not believe—I myself was astounded upon my last visit to Furness to see what my daughter had become. Admittedly it has been over a year, perhaps longer, but . . ." A tremble ran through him. "It is as if she were a changeling and no daughter of my Joanna—a coarse, fat bull, ready for market. Why the animals of my poorest tenants surpass her cleanliness and her manners are those of a . . . I shudder to think of it—the servants shun her and her chambers." He turned back to the decanter and quaffed three more glasses of port in quick succession.

"I must be off to White's," he stated abruptly as he thumped the empty glass down. With a stiff bow he departed as quickly as he had entered, leaving his sister in unhappy thought.

Joanne was nearing her majority—some solution must be found before then, Lady Evelyn realized. A shiver ran through her as she thought of both father and daughter in London; if half the tales concerning the former and all Furness said of the latter were true, London—certainly she, herself—would have a stormy season. But then it would relieve the dreadful news of the rebellion of those bothersome colonies, she thought, and stepped to the looking glass above the slab table. The heartshaped patch on her left cheek was not placed to her liking. . . .

The evening had grown quite late and neither drink nor gambling had freed Lord Furness's mind from the problem nagging at it like a nipping hound. Thumping his hand unsteadily upon the table, he motioned for another bottle of port.

"Wash ye so long in the jaws fer, Furnesh," Lord Blottal asked as the pounding roused him from his drunken slumber. Forcing his bleary eyes to focus, he mumbled, "Ye been no bloody good sport this eve, non 'tal. Mush go. Come, Fontaine." He mauled the man seated next to him, who had also succumbed to the several bottles of port each had imbibed during the evening.

"Fontaine," Blottal said again and pummeled him until he jerked upright. With no further words, merely a haphazard salute, they stumbled away; the two men remaining took no notice of them.

The fourth man at the table, Leonard, Marquess of Wiltham, eyed Furness. A casual observer would have claimed the man had drunk as much as the others, perhaps more by his looks and movements, but the quiet clarity of eye showed a carefully husbanded sobriety.

It had taken Lord Wiltham many months to enter Furness's circle of intimates and, seeing the state of the man now, he wondered if the time had come for his move. Certain of himself, however, he decided to restrain his impatience—so close was he to his objective. An impromptu display of his hand must not destroy what he had worked so diligently to achieve. "My lord, you do appear distressed," he said, leaning toward Furness. "May I not ease your mind? Speak of what troubles you—all that is mine I will press to your aid," he told the other earnestly, thinking ironically of the many duns he had been busily avoiding for weeks.

Furness looked at him over his glass, his mind struggling to sort the words into meaning in his present pickled state. "Education," he finally managed.

"It is important, I suppose," Wiltham noted warily.

"Failed to educate properly."

"Who failed, my lord? Surely not yourself, for your life is ample proof you have not."

"Education," Furness mumbled again.

At a loss, Wiltham asked, "What education, my lord? There are many kinds—that proper to the gentleman, to the soldier, to the gentlewoman . . . of which do you speak?"

Sitting bolt upright, Furness stared at Wiltham, his eyes suddenly focusing sharply. "Many kinds of education. Quite right, you are! The education must suit the purpose," he continued, an idea forming steadily within. "Unusual situation calls for unusual solution! Capital, my man. You have solved my problem." The immediate excitement disappeared from his eyes. "But no. Who? Someone hard and fast on the reins, strong in discipline—mayhap harsh, but effective and most important of all, willing to deal with the problem."

Perplexed, Wiltham could do naught but agree while trying to sort out the meaning.

A brief disturbance drew both men's attention as a club member, drunken and suddenly destitute, became unruly and was "escorted" from White's.

As Furness's vision wandered from the scene, he noticed a table where a group of men were quietly playing whist. "Whittle," he breathed.

Wiltham turned in his chair. "Ah, yes, the Duke of Whittle—I did not realize you were acquainted."

"We are—but vaguely so. I am more known to his brother, Jason Kenton."

"Kenton? Jason Kenton? I do not recall the name or even of hearing of the man."

"There is no wonder in that as he is seldom to London; keeps to himself—stays in that manor of his in Devon most of the year. Has quite a large holding and has turned into a gentleman farmer, I have heard."

"Nicely done by those who have naught else," quipped Wiltham with a meaningful wink at Furness. "Let us drink to the man," he added, refilling the empty glasses. "Then let us go on to better entertainment. This has grown too quiet by far."

The earl took his glass in hand, but did not drink. "I had not thought of Kenton for some time—been years since I've seen the man. Why must be nigh on four and ten years since Warburg."

"Warburg?"

Furness's face relaxed into the smile of remembrance as he explained, "Back in sixty against the French at Warburg—what a day for the cavalry. Proved they were up to snuff.

"Kenton was a young lieutenant in Granby's own regiment—the Blues. Never was a battle more bloody well fought. Kenton was wounded. Shipped back to England shortly after that."

"Sold out after being wounded, eh?" Wiltham asked sarcastically.

"No, not right away. I think his wound left him unfit for service. Married, I think. I've not seen him for four, five years at least. His men had tremendous respect for him—and he was a young man then—always had instant obedience. Yes, instant obedience." He mulled the thought through his mind.

"You were there, my lord, at Warburg? I had no idea you had served in the army," Wiltham said, hoping he wasn't overdoing the awe and that he could distract Furness's mind from this Kenton.

"Tried my hand at it for a time after my wife died— too dull when the war was over," the earl dismissed his words. "Kenton had this idea that I saved his life. Yes, I recall how he promised to repay the favour." He sipped his port slowly. "Methinks the time has come to lay claim to the debt. Why not?" Quaffing the last of his drink, he rose.

"But, my lord, may I not do what you would have this man do?" Wiltham asked.

"Good of you to offer, but no—the more I think on it the better I like it. Must go now; matters to attend to."

"My lord," Wiltham scrambled to his feet, *"Certe* I shall see you tomorrow at Lord Gurley's?"

No answer came back as Lord Furness was well on his way, engrossed with his new scheme for the education of Joanne.

Chapter Two

The Earl of Furness set his face into a disapproving
mask quite unknowingly, straightened his shoulders to
brace himself, and strode into his daughter's bedchamber. The quiver of disgust at the sight of her
was not hidden from Joanne, who answered it by
plopping two more rich sweets into her mouth.

"I have had word from Fordingham."

"To hell with him," came back coldly.

Tightening the check rein on his temper, Furness
advanced to the far side of the bed and surveyed his
daughter. A double chin and heavy jowls, both
smeared with sweets and grime, gave her face the pig-
gish look he despised; her hair, matted and tangled,
was a vermin's nest of vague brown. The once-rich
dressing gown, wrapped haphazardly about her bulky
frame, was stained irrevocably.

Furness could not help thinking of her tiny, delicate
mother. The girl was so unlike her and he had never
liked the squalling brat in infancy. Even then Joanne
had been more a piece of inconvenient property than
a child and, as his neglect and abuse had taken their

toll on her, his disgust had grown. She had not seen her father for the first four years of her life and, when she finally did, it had set the two on a path that had dominated their lives ever since. Joanne at four had not been the tiny reproduction of her mother that Furness expected. He would not allow the child to touch him, and sent her out of his sight after a scorching invective against her looks and being. Scarcely able to understand this encounter then, Joanne had learned its meaning well in the years following.

"I have decided you are to leave Furness."

Joanne eyed him belligerently—suspiciously. She had never been allowed to leave the estate and had long ago accustomed herself to this imprisonment. The certainty of the routine was comforting in its own manner; change was not to her liking.

"I shall have your things packed and arrange for one of my travel coaches to take you—with proper escort, of course."

"Damn to you—I will not leave."

"You have no choice. You will go if I have to have you trussed like a mad dog.

"You are to be taken to Kentoncombe in Devon. Once there, you will be under the authority of the Honorable Jason Kenton—Lord Kenton to you—who is a brother of the Duke of Whittle. He is to see to the correction of your defects—if that is possible. I have written him explaining what I wish. He has authority to do as he sees fit with you and to you.

"If you cooperate and are molded into some semblance of decency, your aunt, Lady Evelyn, has generously offered to sponsor you for the spring season in London. You shall have that one season to achieve a match—I have done all I will in that regard. If Kenton fails to take you in hand or if you fail in your season, I shall be rid of you."

"I'll not leave, damn you." Hatred edged her words.

"This last chance I owe the memory of your mother."

"Mother!" She spat the word venomously.

In an instant he was at the bedside, hurling coverlets, sweets, and books aside, slapping Joanne repeatedly with brutal force. Shaking, he stepped back. "You depart on the morrow—I shall accompany you." As he stepped toward the door he added, "Nothing would please me more than your defiance."

Joanne swallowed deeply as the door slammed shut. Lowering her arms from her face, she gulped. Hatred and anger pressed the tears back as she raised her bulk from the bed and gobbled sweets as fast as she could gather them. These finished, she yanked the bell cord to summon more but no one answered. Stomping to the door ready to loose her pent-up feelings on the first servant she could find, she found the door locked and a fear of old clamped on her heart. Wildly, she glanced about the room, her eyes stopping upon a heap of books. With a shaking hand, she grabbed one and plopped onto her bed, opening the pages, reading hungrily. Her mind fled into the safety of the world of words.

"This is the most amazing dispatch I have ever received," Jason Kenton expostulated. "It would be laughable but for Lord Furness being in earnest," he mused aloud to himself.

Four and ten years had dulled the impetuosity of

youth and at five and thirty, Lord Kenton no longer viewed the Battle of Warburg as he had at the time of its occurrence.

Sitting now in the quiet Devon manor gazing at the somber wooded slope through the window of his study, Jason Kenton had no wish to recall the smoke of cannon fire, or to see the human cannon fodder he, his men, and their horses had trampled over to reach the French. The day had ended in victory and in a permanent, if slight, limp for him. He placed the letter upon the desk before him and gave a wry chuckle. The joke must be on him that he could not recall what Furness had to do with that day so long in the past. Now the man was writing to say he found it necessary to lay claim to the debt owed him. In return for his life, Kenton was to educate Furness's only child in the ways of politeness, obedience, and society.

"He must have gone daft in the head," Lord Kenton said aloud. "I am not a tutor—*certe,* not in the least fitted to the likes of Furness's breed. Why would he want his son rusticating in Devon for eight months? Likely the lad had been kicking his heels a bit too high."

Lord Kenton stretched his frame in the straightbacked chair and stood. Just shy of six feet, his head barely cleared the ceiling and he had to stoop going through the lintel doorway.

Well, it could not harm to let the lad stay a month or so. By that time Furness will have forgiven him, Kenton reasoned as he walked through the corridor. It would not be too great an inconvenience. "Mrs. Caern," he called.

Immediately the mobcapped gray head of his house-keeper popped from a doorway farther down the hall. "Aye, milord?"

"Prepare the coat-of-arms room for a guest—a young lad is going to be staying with us for a time."

"A visitor, milord? That should brighten the coolin' evenin's for ye. When be he a comin'?"

"Soon, I would think, from the tone of the dispatch. No special trouble now—the lad had been in some trouble or other and need not be fussed over."

"Well, ye be the one to show 'im the rights, milord. The room t'will be ready by nightfall."

"Very good. I'm off to check with Tom about those two new heifers."

"Take a wrap if ye be plannin' to be out long," Mrs. Caern called after the lean figure of her master.

While the entire countryside had never quite grown accustomed to seeing Lord Kenton working side by side with his tenants and servants, they had accepted it. It was a source of great pride and fierce loyalty for those connected to Kentoncombe. Mrs. Caern tutted with the rest over his tanned and sinewy arms, weathered face, and hands that did not bespeak the proper gentleman; but none dared voice their opinion near her.

In fact few of his widespread neighbors felt moved to comment overly much on the man, his quiet and industrious ways known to them since his childhood. His face, now as then, was open and friendly, bespeaking an even temper and kindness of heart. Though tanned and marked with maturity, the gentle face had brown eyes that bade a warm welcome to all who stopped by. A shy but ready smile greeted friend and stranger alike. Many had tried and failed to coax him from a life they regarded as dull. His occasional visits to London were not for the pleasure the city could offer to a gentleman of his means, but on purposes of business. He always hurried to return to the peace and beauty of his combe.

This visit may be just what Lord Jason needs, Mrs. Caern ruminated. *Far too quiet he's become. Young blood might stir him a little. Oh, for a wife an' young uns to liven up the place.* Pushing open the windows of the coat-of-arms bedchamber to air it, she saw Lord Jason speaking animatedly with Tom across the yard before the stables.

Ah, a fine man milord is, she thought. *Not strikin' in good looks but comfortin' and easy. It could be hoped this young lad comin' would drag him off to London, Bath, or some such place as the gentry go to find their women—good women,* she amended her thought. *Someplace a fittin' wife could be found for him.*

Chapter Three

The coach never halted longer than necessary to change teams as it made its way from Furness House in Wiltshire toward Devon. Whether there were showers, sunshine, or moonlight pouring down upon them, they proceeded. Lord Furness was obsessed with reaching his goal.

The tearing pace of the cumbersome coach over badly rutted roads and the lack of food and rest were taking their toll upon Lady Joanne. Deprived of the security of her room, her sweets, and her books, she huddled inside the coach, shades drawn, ignoring the view of England's changing countryside.

Spurred by an unseen devil Furness had not allowed the coach to halt for the refreshment of a night's sleep. What sleep he got he took atop the coach, refusing to ride inside with his daughter. For the most part he managed to neither see nor speak with her, allowing only servants to present her what food and drink he thought fit.

The final day of travel arrived at last. Orders were given for the coach to travel at a slower pace while

Furness set off alone. Set upon speaking to Kenton and being off to London before Joanne reached Kentoncombe, he spurred his horse ruthlessly along, halting only at the Pack of Cards, an inn in Combe Martin. There he managed to procure a shave and to wash and make a change of garments. The leisurely pace he set from the inn, so totally opposite to the days before, was calculated to give the proper impression of an unhurried man.

Atop the highest point on the road leading down to Kentoncombe, he halted and scanned the countryside. He had never seen the estate and was amazed that Kenton would be satisfied to spend his life in such a deserted place. Why even the manor is but a miniature of what it should be, he thought distastefully. Turning his eyes to the outer buildings, he saw that they were well kept, neat, and orderly. Apparently satisfied as to the estate's appropriateness for his only child, he urged his steed forward.

Lord Furness clattered into the cobblestone courtyard before the unassuming manor house. A groom ran from the stables to take his horse, imparting the news that the master was in the fields but had been sent for.

The heavy Tudor door before Furness was swung open by a young maid, her neat white mobcap bobbing as she curtsied lowly, as Mrs. Caern had shown her. In the absence of a butler, this noble lady took charge as she appeared behind the maid.

"Milord, I am Mrs. Caern," she greeted the aristocratic-looking man before her. "Lord Kenton will be comin' for a certainty. I seen Tom ridin' to fetch him." The annoyed grimace returned to her by his lordship confirmed her instant dislike of the man. "Come with me, please, milord," she said, showing her disfavour by taking him to the small parlour instead of the larger receiving room reserved for important visitors. With a silent curtsy, she left Lord Furness to himself.

The decanter of port atop a side table came into his vision instantly and he helped himself.

"I am sorry to have kept you waiting," Lord Kenton apologized as his strong strides brought him to the center of the small parlour.

Furness swung around as he insolently emptied his fourth glass of port. "You're here at last. I haven't much time. My coach will be arriving soon and I wish to be gone. Merely stopped to ascertain for myself . . ."

"I will be pleased to have your son spend some time at Kentoncombe," Lord Jason assured him, concealing his surprise at the signs of dissipation and disintegration he saw in the other.

"Son?" Furness cocked his head questioningly as he fingered the large silver buttons on his coat. "Ah . . . I see." He poured and gulped a fifth glassful. "You are willing then, to take my child in hand as I have requested?"

"I am not a tutor, my lord," Lord Kenton said in mild reproof.

"Of course not, man, but I recall how you welded those raw recruits—why all the men respected you. I ask only that you teach my child how to show proper respect—and I care not the means you use—I have found it necessary to lay hands on, myself. Well, I must be off." Furness tossed a bag that landed beside the decanter with a clinking thud. "That should take care of keep—food and all that—new garments, whatever is necessary. Send word to my agent if you need more blunt. I believe March should be early enough for a return to London. I shall send my coach at that time."

Kenton stilled his revulsion as he eyed the bag of coin and watched Furness down yet more port. Doubts were rapidly coming to the fore. "As I said, my lord, your son will be welcome to visit for a time."

Ignoring the words, Furness pulled on his riding gloves and said, "Too bad I couldn't meet your wife, Kenton. Express proper regrets. Good luck to you," he laughed sarcastically, "with my *son*." The last word was swallowed in a nearly mad howl.

No other conversation was exchanged as the two walked through the low corridor and out the door. Once in the saddle, Furness's glinting eyes swept over Kenton and he burst into laughter. "May luck be with you, my lord. I assure you—you will have need of it."

With another mad burst of raucous laughter he spurred his steed from the courtyard, leaving Kenton staring after him wondering what to expect in the son after seeing the father. Furness had not been to his liking in the past; he was even less so now.

Returning to the small parlour, Lord Jason picked up the bag of coin with distaste. *March,* he thought, as he went to his study. He dropped the leather pouch into a drawer of his writing desk, pushing it shut impatiently. His face took on the pensive frown familiar to all who had seen him sort out a problem.

The man actually did not know Morella was dead these thirteen years past. The utter gall of Furness settled upon his mind. *What can I reckon on from the son if the father has proven such a blatant degenerate?* he thought as he returned to his work outdoors.

Lord Furness set the pace at a hard gallop until he came upon his coach. At sight of their approaching master, his men drew to a halt and awaited him.

Orders were quickly given. Lady Joanne was to be deposited upon the doorstep at Kentoncombe and the coach was to depart instantly—thus giving Lord Kenton no choice in the matter when he discovered it was a daughter, not a son with whom he was to deal. There was always the possibility that Kenton would send the chit back in a coach of his own, but Furness was willing to take happenstance.

With a gross chuckle Furness thought of the meeting of his daughter and Kenton. The man will handle it, he mused, dismissing Joanne from his thoughts and turning them to the pleasures that were awaiting him in London. He had been from them far too long.

Joanne heard her father's instructions with an ever-sinking heart. Bruised and battered by every bounce of the coach, denied the consolation of her books, and given meagre meals, her mental state was rapidly deteriorating. She did not know how to deal with the approaching situation. Anger and fear mingled in a stomach-churning battle for supremacy.

Her father's orders indicated Lord Kenton did not wish to fulfill his part of whatever bargain had been struck between the two—but how and why had an arrangement been made? Even in her secluded life, Joanne's reading told her it was a highly improper measure her father had put forward. But she was merely the pawn, with no control of what lay before her. This added to her desperation.

Shakily Joanne raised the coach's shades and gazed at the countryside with a benumbed awareness. The coach slowed and it wended its way up and down hills and around curves. Trees and rock abounded, covering the hilly terrain. Never had she seen such views. For a moment her tension eased.

Taut nerves snapped to the fore as the thud of the team's hooves turned to spark-flinging clinks and stone-echoing crunches as they came upon the crushed-rock approach of Kentoncombe. Accustomed to the grandeur of a large estate such as Furness House, Joanne was shocked by the ramshackle appearance of the small meandering house before which the coach halted. Surely this was merely a renter's cottage, she thought as she viewed the multilevels of slate shingles.

The rattle of the coach's door handle being turned and a shaft of bright light flooding the interior startled her. One of her father's liveried servants stood without, his hand extended to assist her down the steps.

Instinctively she scooted away from him on the seat's edge. The coach had become familiar; beyond it was nothing but the frightening unknown. Was this Kentoncombe after all? Had her father lied—was she to be sold as a farmer's servant girl?

Joanne's heart thumped wildly, her vision blurred, and she gave vent to a piercing scream as she wrapped both hands about the dangling strap at her side.

A word from the scowling servant caused the door on the other side of the coach to be wrenched open. Seeing Joanne's white-knuckled grip upon the strap, the groom left the doorway and returned with a short whip. With a few deft blows of the stock he forced Joanne's fingers to loosen and pushed her toward the other door.

His action caused her to erupt in a frenzy—determined as she was to remain in the coach. The uproar of the three men now pushing, cursing, and tugging at the screaming, clawing girl caused the coach's teams to shift nervously. The commotion drew the attention of those in the house and across the way in the stables.

Despite her bulk and fear-induced strength, the three servants finally managed to drag Lady Joanne from the coach, her baggage tumbling about them as a fifth servant tossed them down. No sooner did the men release their hold than she scrambled to her feet and lunged to return to the coach. While the men heaved her away once again, one shouted orders for the driver to turn the coach about. Joanne's sobbing whine erupted into anguished screams as this was done. With a last desperate attempt she flung herself at the retreating coach, only to trip into a bruising sprawl upon the cobblestone courtyard.

The groom who had given the orders to the driver slapped a letter into the hand of a startled housemaid, who stood gaping in the doorway of the manor, and made a running leap onto the back of the coach as the driver whipped his teams into a run.

Lord Kenton arrived from the stables just in time to catch a last glimpse of the coach with the Furness crest emblazoned upon its sides. His surprise at this hasty departure vanished as he heard "Milord!"

Turning toward the large Tudor entrance of his

manor, he gaped as he saw the mound of flesh, gowned in tattered and soiled remnants, crowned with a filthy matted tangle of hair, from which issued terror-stricken sobs, while the fleshy palms beat upon the cobble-stones.

Chapter Four

Lord Kenton approached the scene calmly. Mrs. Caern had taken the letter from the still-gaping maid and handed it to him as they met at Joanne's side. Staring at her questioningly, he tore open the Furness crest seal and read quickly. Abruptly he rolled the letter and stuck it into his pocket. "We must get her inside," he said above the blubbering from the prone form at their feet. Bending, Lord Kenton touched Lady Joanne gently on the shoulder. Nothing prepared him for her violent reaction.

Joanne rolled onto her side and grabbed his extended hand, sinking her teeth into the flesh at the base of Kenton's thumb. Everyone about the pair stood frozen until blood spurted. The grooms who had rushed forward with fork in hand at the original disturbance stepped forward at the burst of red and thwacked Lady Joanne solidly upon the head.

Unconsciousness came mercifully and freed Lord Kenton's hand for good measure.

Instantly he whipped out his kerchief and wrapped it about the wound, commanding his men to lift

Joanne and carry her inside the manor. Five of them bent to do as ordered. Grumbling, they followed Mrs. Caern as she led the way.

"Gently, his lordship says, ha!" mumbled one.

"How many stone do ye reckon 'er to be?" asked another as he grunted under the burden of her weight.

"The sty be a more fittin' place than one o' 'is lordship's beds," complained a third as they all huffed up a few stairs here and there as they made their way to the coat-of-arms bedchamber.

"Quiet, men."

Lord Kenton's command silenced their tongues.

"Place her on the rug there by the fireplace," he directed when the chamber was reached. "Don't drop her," he said sharply, reading their thoughts. "Now be back to your duties."

"Aye, milord," they nodded as each gave a short bow then shuffled out the door.

"To your duties also," he ordered the three serving girls clustered in the doorway and closed the door upon their noses.

"What's to be done with her, milord? Who is the wench?" Mrs. Caern asked, hands on hips, as she surveyed the hulk of Joanne.

"No wench this, Mrs. Caern, take note. You have before you Lady Joanne, sole child of my lord, the Earl of Furness."

"Loooo," Mrs. Caern covered her mouth in disbelief. "That can't be part of the gentry."

"Nonetheless she is and as such you are to show proper respect."

"But it was the *son* of Furness that was to come."

"So I thought—but my lord Furness . . ." he stopped

and laughed. The elderly housekeeper was like a mother to him, but there were matters of which even she nced not be apprised. "The first thing, I should think, would be a good scrubbing," he noted with a twitch of his nose, changing the subject. "Best be about it while she isn't in her senses—t'would be most safe then I imagine," Kenton added with a lift of his eyebrow as he removed the kerchief from his hand and gave a cursory inspection to the bite.

"Why, milord, let me tend to ye first," Mrs. Caern said, stepping toward him in concern, shocked at her own neglect.

"No, there is little harm done. Lady Joanne nceds your tending far more than this. But be wary. Call mc as soon as she begins to waken. Her eyes were rolling white, mad as any battle-crazed man I've ever seen.

"Get her as clean as you can and find a clean night-dress in her baggage—I'll have it sent up directly." He looked down at the quiet form as if she were a wounded creature. "If you women cannot get her abed, cover her and have the men aid you. Burn the garments she now wears." He went to the door. "Let me know when you have her abed or if she shows signs of awakening. I will be in my study." After a last pitying glance, he departed.

The three serving girls fairly well tumbled into the room when Mrs. Caern went to call them. As they righted themselves, they were peppered with orders.

"Meg, fetch me scissors and soap—the strongest we have—and a brush from the scullery.

"Nell, hot water and aplenty of it.

"Ann, a tub, cloths from the linen hold for washing and drying. To it," she snapped at the staring trio.

They scampered to their appointed errands and Mrs. Caern returned to Lady Joanne's side. Kneeling, she felt for and found a strong pulse. The girl before her presented as disgusting a sight and smell as Mrs. Caern had ever encountered, but she could not suppress the twinge of growing compassion. *An earl's daughter,* she thought. *How had the poor thing come to this state?*

Meg stumbled to a halt beside her, holding forth the scissors and soap she had been sent for.

Rolling up her sleeves, Mrs. Caern took the scissors and starting at the sleeve edge, began cutting through.

Jason Kenton reread Lord Furness's letter slowly, then lay it upon the desk top before him. The calm brown of his eyes was disturbed by flickering sparks of anger. Now he understood Furness's spell of mad humour. The man must be mad—no, worse—lower than an animal to send his daughter to a man he knows little of but for a chance meeting four and ten years past, he thought. *I could be a rake.* But thinking of Lady Joanne's form, he dismissed that trend of thought.

However a mental vision of the lady now in the coat-of-arms bedchamber stimulated further contemplation. Why was she delivered in such a manner? Obviously this sojourn was not to her liking.

Lord Jason fingered the bandage upon his hand. Strong jaws and teeth, if no other attributes were hers. Was she then *non compos*? That idea was discarded immediately. Furness would have simply locked her away forever if that were the case. He leaned forward, his forearms resting upon the desk top, the anger within turning to concentration. The smell of the lady he could easily understand, reminiscing briefly upon his experiences with the cosseted nobility. Even a degree of uncleanliness would have been fathomed—bathing not being yet a national habit—but account for the dilapidation of her person and dress, and her behaviour! What was he to do? Kenton pondered seriously.

A man who by habit weighed problems carefully, Lord Jason did not, as Furness expected, immediately think of Joanne's removal, although the reason was not what Furness would have expected. Very simply, Kenton had a weakness for the injured, the hurt, and clearly saw that Joanne's state, at least her mental state, would be worsened by any further removal.

No, he reasoned, we shall wait. Compassion as well as curiosity as to the "why" of her condition would ensure Lady Joanne's stay beyond this day.

The enclosed room, the heated water, and the difficulty of dealing with Joanne's unconscious weight had reduced Mrs. Caern and the three serving girls to perspiration-drenched figures. Damp mobcaps sagged over wet wisps of hair as sweat trickled down their brows, but Lady Joanne's flesh now had a rare scrubbed freshness and her hair, though lying with dull lifelessness, was cleaned of most of its vermin and brushed free of the tangling and matting, albeit not without cost.

"What's to be done with this?" Meg asked, staring disgustedly at the heap of offensive hair that had once been Joanne's.

"Into the fire with it—along with all the other things," Mrs. Caern commanded as she worked with the other two struggling valiantly to pull the night-dress onto the unhelpful figure of their ministrations.

With a collective sigh they all sat back staring at their accomplishment.

"Be it not odd she's not to 'er senses yet, ma'am?" Nell asked.

"Her breathin' be good—I'll not be concerned, yet. Let's roll her onto that clean sheet and get her to the bed. Lord Kenton will likely be wondering what we're about so long," the housekeeper noted, shuffling to her knees and rising tiredly.

"It's beyond me how this can be a 'lady,'" Meg commented sharply as she put her weight into the task of moving Joanne.

"It's not yers to be knowin', or even thinkin' on—keep yer thinkin' to yerself. This day's work is to go no further," snapped Mrs. Caern as she gave each girl a hard-eyed stare. "We don't know what's to come of this, so beware and answer no questions. Lord Kenton will not have a guest gabbled about."

The three nodded reluctantly, what little joy there had been in the task now taken from them. Stoically they struggled, pulling, pushing, and finally heaving with all their might until Lady Joanne lay abed.

The flickering of the unconscious girl's eyelids caught Mrs. Caern's keen sight as she tucked a fresh sheet over her. "Quickly, girls, clear the chamber.

"Nell, fetch Lord Kenton. He said he would be in his study. Tell him the lady is awakening."

"Aye, mum," Meg answered and scurried out of the chamber.

Lord Kenton halted to allow Nell and Ann to exit, their arms filled with soiled towels, before he entered.

Finished with straightening the bedcovers, Mrs. Caern watched Lord Jason as he approached the bedside, then stood gazing down. The harsher emotions did not often show themselves upon his features, but she could clearly read anger upon them now.

"Bruises—it was bruises not dirt that covered her face," he said slowly to himself. "Are there such marks over the rest of her?" Kenton asked, still staring at the girl.

"Aye, milord—but more than likely they were caused by the journey . . ." Her voice trailed off, the conclusion being apparent.

"His own daughter," he murmured, then faced his housekeeper. "I was told she was regaining her senses."

"Yes, milord, see how the eyelids flutter—a sure sign 'twill not be long before they open," she explained. "I felt you would wish to be here."

"Quite right. Finish bringing the chamber to rights. I shall watch her for a time." He took a chair and moved it closer to the bed, sat, and began studying Joanne's features. Behind him the housekeeper mustered the three girls, along with two men they had recruited from the gardens, to remove the water-filled tub and the last of the towels. With a last glimpse of her silent, pondering master, Mrs. Caern closed the chamber door silently, the work within completed.

A low moan escaped Lady Joanne as she shifted uneasily in the soft feather bed. Seeing the beads of perspiration across her brow, Lord Kenton rose and opened the windows of the chamber, allowing the cooler breeze of early evening to enter. He was one of the few who believed fresh air more beneficial than harmful to the ill. The sun had set but full light still abounded as he looked across the waving treetops surrounding the manor.

Joanne's eyes fluttered open, closed, and then remained open as he returned to the bedside. Her mind could not grasp where she was, only that her head ached horribly and her skin felt as if it had been flayed; her entire body was raw and irritated and an odor that was totally alien prevailed about her.

The man gazing down at her smiled and she wondered who he could be and why he was smiling at her. *I am dreaming again,* she thought. Closing her eyes, she drifted into the sleep of the exhausted.

At least she appears to be rational now, Kenton mentally noted. *When she awakens, I shall have to assess the situation. A visit with the Lady Joanne should prove interesting. . . .*

Chapter Five

The moon melted into the horizon and the sun pushed over the edge; still Lady Joanne did not awaken. As his concern mounted Lord Kenton sent for Dr. Fowler from Ilfracombe.

Mrs. Caern frowned as she led the young man who answered the summons to Lord Kenton's study. "Dr. Ames, milord," she announced as his lordship turned from his desk.

"That will be all," Lord Kenton dismissed the housekeeper. "I was expecting Dr. Fowler," he began, studying the young physician, noting with approval the man's unpretentious long blue coat, plain white breeches, and modest periwig.

"I am just recently come from London—to study with Dr. Fowler," Ames explained. "He had a very bad night—his gout, you know—and wished me to come in his place," he continued, his gaze unwavering. "He did ask me to tell you that he had received a letter from his son in the Colonies giving details of the evacuation of Boston in March and telling that they are readying for action. There is every sign the colonials are going to go through with the threatened declaration of independence." Ames shifted uneasily. "Dr. Fowler emphatically insisted I say that Burgoyne is being sent to join General Howe and that they will teach the damned ingrates a lesson."

"Do you favour the king's position in this war, Dr. Ames?" Kenton asked out of curiosity.

The physician paused, assessing his answer. "In truth, my lord, I favour Mr. Burke and Mr. Fox's opinion in the matter and consider it unfortunate that Lord North is unable to persuade His Majesty from the present course." He finished with cautious certainty, wondering if his words would bring dismissal.

"I am of like mind," Kenton agreed. "Thank Dr. Fowler for the information and tell him I will call to get all the particulars. But another question, Doctor. Do you believe in letting blood in the majority of cases you attend?"

An eagerness came to the young physician's eye. "No. I believe the current practice of bleeding a patient no matter what his malady oft increases the danger of death. The use of leeches and cupping in many cases, if not harmful, is ineffective. Dr. John Hunter, the noted surgeon in London, recommends against it. Why he . . ."

"I agree—totally." Kenton smiled at the other's enthusiasm for the subject. "But let me call Mrs. Caern. I wish you to examine a guest. Lady Knolls arrived yesterday and was victim of an accident which rendered her unconscious. She has not regained her senses since. Please assess her condition."

* * *

"Lord Kenton," Dr. Ames announced his return to the study.

"Please close the door, Doctor," Kenton said, rising. "A glass of wine?"

"No, thank you, my lord. I have many calls to make before this eve and prefer a clear head," Dr. Ames answered crisply.

"As you wish," noted Lord Kenton, pleased at this outlook of the man. "Be seated, please. What did you find?" he asked, coming directly to the point.

"The young lady in question is not ill as far as I can ascertain. The lack of details adds to the difficulty, you understand. But, although there is no fever or other adverse symptoms, her general health is very poor. The condition of her legs indicates little exercise—I would venture to say there is even a lack of sufficient walking. Her skin tone and weight all indicate poor diet.

"Now, there is a bump from a blow on the head but no other damage. Her sleep is common to those who have done without any for several days. I would venture that she will awaken on the morrow—weakened perhaps, but unharmed," the young doctor concluded, peering sharply at Lord Kenton to assess his reaction. The bruises he would not mention without his lordship bringing them up first, but the reputation of this man implied that he was not responsible for them.

"What recommendations would you have for improving her health?" Kenton questioned, leaning back in his chair.

"Nothing that your own common sense cannot recommend, my lord. Fresh air, plenty of exercise. I realize that activity is generally frowned upon for young ladies, my lord, but I have found it to be of good consequence among my patients. Also good food, but not in excess." Dr. Ames wondered at the question but answered it, restraining his curiosity beyond asking, "Your guest will be remaining with you for some time?" He waved the question aside with his own hand. "I did not wish to pry into your affairs, my lord—but it would be wise if the young lady did remain for at least a few days—until she recovers her strength."

"I agree totally, Dr. Ames. Have no fear," Lord Kenton said, rising and extending his hand. "Thank you for coming. Since you are new to our area, may I extend my welcome. Feel free to stop in whenever your calls bring you near the manor."

"Why, thank you, Lord Kenton," the surprised young man answered. "I will be most happy to return if you feel it is necessary. If you wish, I shall stop by in a few days to see your guest's progress."

"I do not think that will be necessary, but feel free to do so if you have doubts as to her recovery," Lord Kenton answered, smiling as he led the way to the door. "May I ask about your former patients? You speak of them with such warmth."

Dr. Ames blushed slightly, then raised his head defensively. "Before coming to Dr. Fowler I studied and worked at the Children's Hospital in London."

"I am certain they miss you," returned his lordship. "Please give my regards to Dr. Fowler." Lord Kenton bade Ames farewell at the door. Walking back to his study, he repeated, "Fresh air, exercise, and good food—all of which we have aplenty here at Kentoncombe."

Clanging and clattering of metal accompanied by rising voices drew Lord Jason abruptly from deep sleep, his first thought being that he was back at Warburg. He jumped from his bed not fully awake. The cool, smooth oak beneath his bare feet and the vague light of dawn belied that location but the faint tumult continued.

With a jaw-stretching yawn he drew on his breeches and sought the source of the noise. It was soon apparent that the commotion was coming from the coat-of-arms bedchamber. His guest had apparently awakened and not with the calm disposition he had anticipated. Forgoing further clothing, Lord Kenton dashed into the corridor and sprinted past the four doors of the chambers between his and the coat-of-arms. A loud crash against the door halted his immediate entry.

Cautiously he opened the door during a lull in the action within.

Nell saw him. "Milord, thanks be to God," she breathed in relief and then ducked as Lady Joanne threw another of the armorial shields that hung upon the far wall of the bedchamber. Sheathed swords, wrenched from their hanging places, littered the floor along with the shields already removed.

Beleaguered, Meg was striving valiantly to get close enough to Joanne to seize her, although what she would do after that had not occurred to her.

Briefly Lord Jason thought the scene resembled too

plainly a pair of hunting dogs who had cornered a prey beyond their capabilities. The humour of this passed quickly as he realized that "prey" was exactly what Joanne felt herself to be. Her looks and movements were those of the unthinking, the panicked.

"Meg, Nell," his voice rang out clearly, "out—I shall deal with this."

Both girls looked at their master askance but dashed for the door he held open.

"Good morn, my lady," Lord Kenton addressed Lady Joanne calmly as he gave the door a push to close it. "We are pleased to see you have awakened in such 'spirit.'" He smiled, stepping very slowly toward her.

Panting from her exertions, Joanne leaned against the wall, a small shield in her hands. Something about the man before her was familiar and his calm appearance and voice had a momentary subduing effect.

When a few feet from Joanne, Kenton held out his hand. "The shield," he said. "It must be uncomfortable to hold. Let me rehang it for you."

Joanne's eyes followed his hand and then went down to the shield she held. Her mind grasped for a decision which came abruptly as she spied him take a step. Fearing he was about to grab her, she screamed, "No!" and heaved the shield at him.

It caught Lord Jason off guard, but he managed to catch it, stepping away from her as he did. "My lady, I fear you dislike this interruption."

The words caused Joanne, who was tearing frantically at another shield on the wall, to turn slowly and face him. She had expected the man to lay hold of her and was surprised to see that he was walking slowly back to the door of the chamber.

"I shall leave you until you have recovered," he continued calmly. "You shall find your garments have been unpacked—perhaps you wish to find a dressing gown. I shall return in a short while." With a smile and a bow he left.

The click of the door caused Joanne to burst forward and pull on the handle. She gasped as it opened easily.

"You wish something, my lady?" Lord Kenton asked, only to find the door slammed in his face.

Inside the chamber Joanne leaned against the door, but no one tried to re-enter, and when she cautiously pulled once more it still came open easily. It had not been locked as she had feared. Secure in that knowledge, she left it and stepped over the articles strewn about the room where Mrs. Caern's order had reigned so shortly before.

The strangeness of her surroundings began returning to her senses and she went to the windows, drawing back the curtains to allow full light to enter.

The bedchamber faced the east and the reddish glow of the sun above the surrounding treetops bespoke a warm July day in the offing. A soft rose light illuminated the chamber, and turning from the wooded view before her Joanne took in what she thought to be her new prison.

Due to the collection of armorial shields on the far wall, the chamber was known as the coat of arms. Second in size only to the master's bedchamber, it was a large room which held the size of its decorations easily. Despite the damage Joanne had done in her panic and fury upon awakening in unknown surroundings, the chamber's cleanliness and sense of order astounded her. The unfamiliar odor of lemon and beeswax and the glossy shine of the dark, rich wood paneling and floor assailed her sight and smell. Her eyes traveled from the deep-toned shimmer of the dark paneling of the walls to the Elizabethan frieze. A few swords and shields still hung in their proper places upon the far wall, and upon the west wall a massive wardrobe, ornately carved, stood a brief distance from the huge, posted, draped bed. The reflection of the dawn's rays enhanced its beauty as the light gleamed off the cut surfaces. The last sputterings of a candle drew her eyes to the elaborate gilded sconces upon the third wall with their reflective mirrors and a large gilded, wrought-iron family crest that hung between them. Joanne gave only a cursory examination to these, her main thoughts being that she must have gone farther, for this was not the farmer's cottage she had been brought to. With a heavy sigh she trod back to the bed and drew back the remainder of the curtains before sitting down upon it. Fatigue assailed her and she lay back; her eyes closed and she slept once more.

Returning to his guest's chamber after having dressed, Lord Jason tapped lightly on the door and opened it slowly. The soft pink light flooding the room lay gently over Joanne, giving her face the healthy hue it lacked on its own and somewhat diminishing the discolorations. Pleased to find her asleep, Lord Jason gazed awhile, then smiled and withdrew. Humming a gay ditty, he went down for breakfast. The education of Joanne had begun.

Chapter Six

The manor house was unnaturally quiet to Lord Jason when he entered near midday. Having seen to the work schedule, he had turned his mind toward his guest and determined to visit with her.

"Mrs. Caern," he called out. In answer came a resounding crash of plates and silver followed closely by the higher-pitched crash of glassware. All issued from the floor above. This time no thought was needed to decide from whence the disturbance came. Lord Kenton bounded the few steps along the winding way to the coat-of-arms chamber. Vile epithets sounded through the door and Mrs. Caern trod upon his lordship's feet when she exited from the chamber that Lord Kenton attempted to enter.

"Truly, milord, you cannot expect us to serve the likes of her. Why the chamber is a shambles," Mrs. Caern protested vehemently.

"I shall see to her," he strove to calm the elderly woman. "Fetch a tray of tea and toast for Lady Joanne and a cold collation for myself," he ordered, seeking to occupy her mind, thus distracting it from its distress.

"But milord, she will only . . ." the housekeeper began in protest.

"Have one of the serving girls bring it if you fear for yourself."

A glint appeared in her eye at the challenge. "Tea and toast, aye, milord," Mrs. Caern answered with smarting crispness. With head up and shoulders straight she stepped briskly down the corridor.

A half-smile followed her briefly before Lord Kenton turned and faced the half-opened doorway. His knock on the door frame brought a crash as Joanne slammed the door in answer.

What was it Furness wanted taught? Ah, obedience and respect, mused Lord Kenton, opening the door slowly. The latter was certainly lacking. "How good of you to bid me enter." He greeted Joanne with a smile.

A candlestick, hurtled at him from her ladyship's hand, was her greeting.

Catching it deftly, Kenton noted smoothly, "It is a bit early to have need of light—perhaps you mean you have no wish for it after the sun has retired? I will be pleased to return it to you upon your *request.*"

The emphasis upon the last word, indeed the man's demeanour, confused Joanne. Having seen only her father and those select debauched few he allowed to come to Furness House, she had no means of judging the likes of Kenton. His manner was not that of a servant and yet the simplicity of the brown knit breeches, the tall boots, a simple shirtfront and stock beneath the smooth-fitting coat, did not meet the standards set by her father's intimates.

"I demand you take me to your master—I wish a coach immediately," she ordered, her voice rising toward hysteria.

"You are my guest and I would be considered a very bad host if I were to turn you out after such a brief visit, my lady. Why, you are hardly in a state to travel," he added, motioning at her degree of undress—the linen nightdress alone swathing her figure.

"I have sent for tea and toast for you, my lady. If you wish to dress we could partake of it on the north terrace. It is quite a pleasant view and well shaded," Lord Kenton offered.

"Tea and toast," spluttered Joanne. "You call that food—I am famished! I demand food—beef, mutton—at once."

"Demand. Such a word does not become a lady—as well as a few others I have heard issue from you, but I suppose we have your father to thank for that. As soon as we have imposed some order in your behaviour we shall have to see to your words," Kenton said as if to himself, his smile increasing.

"Order in my behaviour—my words. Who are you to think to order me? I am the daughter of an earl and you must do as I say," she bluffed.

"I heartily doubt that I shall," he tossed back lightly. "No, indeed, it must be the other way for benefit of you—you must learn."

"You . . . I will . . . report you to your master. Out of my chamber at once. How dare you to enter without my permission." She swung about, searching for a loose object with which to make her point.

Ignoring her words and actions, Lord Jason walked to the windows and opened them.

"I will catch my death," Joanne howled and dashed to close them. "Don't you know a draft has the worst consequences."

"I beg to differ, my lady," Kenton returned, reaching to reopen the windows. "Fresh air is what the constitution needs and these windows are to remain open." His smile returned as he observed her reaction; he could almost hear her blasting thoughts.

Accustomed to screaming and physical violence with any command, Joanne was uncertain how to view this tormentor who spoke calmly, firmly, and with the authority to make his bidding followed ringing in his voice. Her consternation grew as he ignored her and surveyed the bedchamber.

"It is evident that this chamber is not to your taste," he said slowly, his expression very serious. "Therefore I will have all embellishments removed until such time as you can see to at least tolerate their presence," Kenton told Joanne, turning back to face her. "You are my guest and I wish to give all the conveniences at the command of Kentoncombe—for your enjoyment, not for your abuse."

Joanne did not note the hardening of the voice on the last phrase. Her mind had become keyed to the word *Kentoncombe*. "Then I am where he made arrangements to put me after all," the young woman said, bitterness filling every word. "And you are Lord Kenton?" she asked with a sharp edge to her voice.

Bowing, he acknowledged the fact.

"You do not seem to be of my father's ilk—what

has he promised you to keep me prisoner?" Joanne asked, her anger flaming once more.

"First," the steely voice belied the smile, "you are my guest—not my prisoner. Free to come and go as you choose. Secondly, Lord Furness has no hold upon me, now, nor ever will. I suggest you enjoy your visit here—no matter what its duration."

"If I am free to go, why have you not ordered a coach to return me to Furness House?"

"I do not deem that wise. You need rest—to recover from the rigours of the journey here. We are not formal in our manner here and have few visitors—you could be a welcome guest."

A knock at the door interrupted them. "Enter," called Lord Kenton.

Mrs. Caern pushed the door open cautiously. Disapproval covered her features even more deeply as she saw his lordship casually standing with the "lady" dressed only in her bedgown. Did the girl have no decency?

Bearing laden trays, Meg and Nell followed, eager to catch a glimpse of the scene.

"Take those to the north terrace," Lord Kenton ordered crisply, stepping forward.

"No!" shouted Joanne, her eyes bright upon the sight of the cold beef, biscuits, and other foods upon Meg's tray. She moved forward to grab the tray but his lordship's hold upon her arm stayed her. When she made to pull it from him she found the second one a prisoner.

"To the terrace," snapped Lord Kenton.

Joanne erupted into a writhing, kicking, screaming mass.

The serving girls and Mrs. Caern left with all haste, the girls gazing fearfully over their shoulders and Mrs. Caern thinking this was only justice for his lordship's lenience.

"Bring back that food! I demand it!"

"My lady, to demand is to receive nothing," Lord Kenton tried to tell her while staying out of striking distance of her feet. "To ask politely is to receive everything."

Her anger fogging her senses, Joanne did not listen. From attacking she turned to trying to escape.

Sensing the change, Kenton released his hold and she dashed to the bed, heaved herself atop it and dissolved into sobs.

When the blubbering slackened, he told her, "Since you choose not to break your fast, I suggest you dress and take a walk about the grounds. You may join me for supper if you wish this eve—I shall have someone summon you at the proper time." Kenton had walked to the door as he spoke and paused to add, "We do not dress formally here, as you may have noted. A day dress would be adequate this eve. Till then, my lady." Bowing at the broad back, he left.

Mrs. Caern awaited him on the terrace. She poured his tea as he sat. "Milord, I must speak," she began.

"That will not be necessary," Kenton answered. "I know this is a trial for you and all the servants but one you must bear. There is no choice." His look confirmed his words.

"Aye, milord," she answered tiredly, "but . . ."

"Resign yourself—matters shall improve. Now," he opened his napkin and placed it in his lap, "this afternoon while Lady Joanne is out of her chamber or asleep strip the room of everything. Leave only the bed and the wardrobe. Speak with the members of the household and instruct them to avoid her ladyship. I wish no one to speak with her until I give permission."

"Aye, milord." The gray head shook quizzically as it acknowledged the orders.

"Also, Lady Joanne is to be given nothing to eat without my approval—no order of hers is to be obeyed."

"But, milord . . ."

"Mrs. Caern, in all of our years together I have never heard so many buts. You have not questioned the wisdom of my actions in the past."

"If that is all, milord," she said as he paused, "I shall return to my work."

A nod gave dismissal and Lord Kenton settled back in his chair. Neither the bright reds, yellows, and purples of the summer blooming flowers edging the terrace nor the tempting food on the tray before him caught his attention. He seemed to be staring at the sculptured shrubbery just beyond the terrace backed by the formal gardens, but his mind was fastened onto the last two conversations he had just completed.

Realizing he had unconsciously made the commitment to try to "civilize" the young woman, he wondered how it had come about. That question was soon overrun by the desire to learn more of her and the cause of her plight. *If only there were some way to fathom the reasons behind her actions,* he thought. Her upbringing was strangely lacking, for she felt no need for nor displayed any ladylike modesty, and yet he felt that innocence lay behind that. Her treatment of the servants, of—everything—was abominable. But

. . . he paused. But there was a reason for it all, her actions were not done from spite but through a lack of knowledge of any other way to behave—of this he felt certain. Most clearly he sensed an unsubdued bitterness about her; the look of fear, more often than not covered by anger, hovered always in the depths of her eyes. He could not turn her away.

Furness's note had made it clear that Furness House would be forbidden the girl, and if he arranged to have her sent to London in her present state the girl would be the laughing stock of all.

It was impossible to turn the child out—to put her upon the mercies of the likes of Furness. Kenton sighed and straightened in his chair. Perhaps he had uncannily taken the right direction. He hoped it was the proper course of action. But could he educate Joanne to the ways of polite society?

Chapter Seven

A week had passed—the longest week in Mrs. Caern's memory. Waiting for the next explosion filled the manor and the minds of all except Lord Kenton. The elderly housekeeper did not know if she should take pride in his lordship's restraint and calmness or view it as early lunacy.

About Lady Joanne Mrs. Caern was not undecided. Never had such a willful, arrogant, utterly spoiled tormentor been ensconced at Kentoncombe. If there were no improvement soon, Mrs. Caern would not blame the servants for taking their leave, as a few had been heard to threaten in low mumbles.

Joanne's adjustment to her new regimen was nonexistent at this point. At the moment this was being brought painfully home to Lord Kenton.

Screeches and screams had alerted Kenton of the latest outburst of his guest. Alone in his study, he indulged in a frown, something hidden from everyone at Kentoncombe. Sadly he admitted to having made not even the smallest progress with the girl. Not true, his humourous side prompted—she has eaten little since her arrival. A smile did appear at that thought. Since the meals she received were based on good behaviour, there would have been none except for the bending of the premise. It was discernible to the studious eye that the seams of Joanne's gowns, though still strained, were no longer in danger of bursting.

But this was the only hopeful note in the entire dirge, Kenton thought sadly. A breakthrough must be found or I will be forced to admit defeat before I am properly begun.

His lordship's head was jerked about as he realized the commotion, rather than dying out, had come close to his doors. Before he could rise, the door to his study was thrown open and a hapless Nell was shoved in by a livid Lady Joanne.

"What is the meaning of this?" Lord Kenton asked calmly, the hardening of his eyes alone betraying his anger.

"You will instruct this wench to answer me when I question her," Joanne shouted at him.

"You are not to raise your voice, my lady," he said. "Nell, return to your duties," Kenton told the shaken girl as he helped her rise.

"No! She will go when I dismiss her!"

With a reprimanding glance at Joanne, Lord Kenton took Nell's hand and led her to the door. "Go on—I shall see this does not happen again," he said reassuringly. "Go on, everything is all right."

"You have no right to treat me like this—order that girl back at once."

A stonefaced, silent glare answered her.

"I'll get her then," Joanne snapped and stepped forward.

Kenton blocked the way.

"Stand aside!" Unthinking, Joanne slapped him across the face.

The features barely twitched beneath the livid red patch raised by the blow.

His non-reaction produced a startling effect. Confusion battled with rage. "What is wrong with you?" Joanne challenged. "Can you never act . . . right? Why do you never show anger?" Tears of frustration streamed down her cheeks. If there had been a way to flee, she would have taken it; instead she was forced to face his lordship, still barring her way to the door.

Kenton's stoic look and silence fanned Joanne's sinking ire. A stream of vile epithets that showed she had been giving no little amount of her idle time to the subject poured out. At last, breathless and choked by half-sobs, she ended, "Damn you. Can you not speak? Why will no one speak to me? In my father's house at least they spoke to me." Pleading had entered her voice. "Speak to me!" The lack of response spurred her and, grabbing a bisque figurine from a nearby table, she hurled it at Kenton, who did not move. "Are you not human?" Joanne asked through her tears as she stepped closer. "Speak to me or I'll bring this room to shambles!"

Lord Kenton still stood quiet and unmoving. In a last burst of frenzy Joanne pummeled at his chest. "Why? Why do you torment me?" she sobbed as her blows grew weaker. "You must speak to me." Frantic, she grabbed the collar of Kenton's jacket, "Or at least let me send for my books."

No flicker of any emotion crossed Kenton's face.

"What does it take? Tell me! Please!" she breathed,

her head sagging and her arms dropping to her sides.

Her last word was like a magic incantation. Kenton whipped his kerchief from his pocket, and putting an arm consolingly about Joanne's shoulder used the other to raise her face and gently wipe the tears away. "My lady," he said softly, "I have always been open to conversation with you—but you must learn to speak other than orders or demands. As for books, you may have all you desire from my own library, only for the asking—it is quite a complete selection, you will find, I believe."

The tortured girl knew not what to make of this new tenderness in the man's eyes or the gentleness of his touch, for she had experienced neither from anyone before.

"Come." He guided her to a chair. "I will pour you some Madeira—it will calm your nerves. Use this to dry your eyes." He placed his kerchief in her hands.

Suppressing his feeling of triumph, Lord Kenton returned to Joanne's side and took a seat in a chair beside hers. He pressed the goblet of wine into her hands. "Drink this, please, my lady."

Slowly the glass was raised to her lips; a sip was swallowed. The raised eyes caught sight of Kenton's pleased smile. "I hate you," she said simply and flung the remainder of the wine in his face.

His lordship retrieved his kerchief from her hand and dabbed his face dry, a more stoic expression replacing the smile.

That bright smile now wreathed Joanne's face as she sat, her hands folded docilely in her lap.

A timid knock at the door turned Lord Kenton's

head, but not before he saw the girl tense, her fingers quickly clenched together.

Cautiously Mrs. Caern opened the door, just enough to allow her to see inside. "You have a visitor, milord," she informed him, jerking her head meaningfully at Lady Joanne.

Lord Kenton followed the motion with a wry grin. "Who is it, Mrs. Caern?"

"That young Dr. Ames who called a week past."

"Ah, yes. Show him in at once. I believe he will be delighted at your progress, my lady," he smiled at Joanne, while thinking to himself, *if only she can remain seated without flinging anything at the good doctor.*

"Your lordship, I am happy you were free to receive me," Dr. Ames said, genuinely pleased at the opportunity to visit. He stopped short when he saw Lady Joanne and bowed deeply.

Lord Kenton rose and stepped to his side. "Lady Joanne, may I present Dr. Ames.

"Dr. Ames, this is Lady Joanne Knoll—of the House of Furness."

"This is indeed a great honour and privilege, my lady," Dr. Ames told the somewhat startled girl—unaccustomed as she was to such an introduction and the young man's obvious attention. "And most pleased to see your recovery has been both rapid and complete," he added sincerely. "It is not always one finds patients who are willing to follow my advice as you evidently have."

Having no idea what the doctor was speaking of

but responding to the genuine concern in his voice and manner, Joanne smiled and nodded.

"Dr. Ames was kind enough to examine you after your unfortunate accident on the day of your arrival," Lord Kenton threw in as a partial explanation.

"And yours also?" Joanne asked with the lift of an eyebrow.

"Join us for a glass of wine?" Kenton asked, ignoring her words. "Ah, I recall," he said, before the physician could make sense of the sudden change, "you wish to have a clear head for your patients. Some lemonade then—or tea?"

"Lemonade would quench my thirst," Dr. Ames responded, deciding it best to ignore her ladyship's words as his lordship had done but curious of the underplay between them.

"Mrs. Caern, please bring three glasses of lemonade," Lord Kenton said to the elderly woman, who had not budged from the doorway. It took a further reassuring nod from his lordship to send her on her way.

"Take a chair, Dr. Ames—we are not high on formality here, as I have told you."

"Dr. Ames?"

Both men's attention turned to Lady Joanne, the one politely interested, the other hopeful but concerned.

"I was wondering if you were required to read Hippocrates' works during your studies?" Lady Joanne asked, noting with supreme pleasure the look of surprise on her host's features.

"Hippocrates? Why I . . . I do not mean to appear presumptuous, my lady, but what can a gentle person of your kind know of the man?" Dr. Ames asked.

"I read Greek, Latin, and French fluently, Doctor." Her head rose proudly. "I . . . I have not been overly occupied at my home and reading fills much of my time. Have you read his work?" she pursued.

A low blush came to the young man's features. "I must admit I have not, although I know of his philosophy toward his patients. I subscribe to it, of course. As a matter of fact, one could say it inspired my coming to see Lord Kenton," he said turning momentarily to his host. Swinging his attention back to Lady Joanne, he asked enthusiastically, "Would you consider discussing Hippocrates with me if I should call again? I will speak to Dr. Fowler and see if he has a copy of the work in his library, but I would need your aid—my knowledge of Greek being limited."

A lull in the conversation ensued as Mrs. Caern returned to serve the lemonade herself; evidently no one was taking a chance with Lady Joanne, even with his lordship and Dr. Ames present.

"With Lord Kenton's permission I would be pleased to help you, Doctor," reached Kenton's unbelieving ears as he closed the doors behind Mrs. Caern.

"If it pleases you to do so, my lady, I can find no objection," he returned, giving Joanne a light bow. Seating himself he asked, "You mentioned having a purpose to your visit, Dr. Ames?"

"Yes, your lordship. Of course I was anxious to see how Lady Knoll had progressed," he said smiling at Joanne, "but I must admit to further motive. Some business I need to discuss with you, my lord."

Kenton nodded for him to continue, but a look of distress crossed the doctor's features.

"We can go to the library if you wish," Lord Kenton offered.

Noting Lady Joanne's smile wane, Dr. Ames hastened to reassure her. "It is not that I wish to be from your presence, my lady, merely that the topic I wish to discuss with Lord Kenton would be distressful to a gentlewoman such as yourself. I beg you to excuse us."

There was no denying the young doctor's honesty. "Of course, Dr. Ames. It is kind of you to be so concerned," Joanne answered, shifting her eyes to Kenton upon the last word. She rose and extended her hand. "It is a pleasure to have met you. Please do call again."

The startled doctor had jumped to his feet as Joanne rose and extended his hand only after looking to Lord Kenton for approval to do so. Giving her hand a gentle squeeze, he bowed over it. "The pleasure, most assuredly, was mine," he said.

"There will be no need for you to depart," she said haughtily to Lord Kenton. "I shall go to my chamber."

"A walk in the gardens would be much better at this time of day, my lady," Kenton bantered back.

"Yes, yes," threw in the doctor.

"Until next we meet, Doctor," Joanne said with a flickering smile. As Ames bowed to her once again, she stuck her tongue out at Lord Kenton and strode from the room.

"How delightful she is," the doctor noted after Joanne's departure.

"Ah, well, yes," Lord Kenton agreed after making a mental reservation as to the adjective. "What is it you wished to speak of?" he asked, curious to know what this young man had on his mind that would prove distressful to Joanne. Thus far the lady had shown herself much better at giving distress than experiencing it herself.

Chapter Eight

Confidence temporarily deserted Dr. Ames. He gulped half his lemonade. Across the small space separating them he watched Lord Kenton patiently sipping from his glass.

"You mentioned your work at the Children's Hospital on your last visit," his lordship said, hoping to ease the young doctor into his purpose. "Do you miss working with youngsters now that you have a greater variety among your patients?"

"Most curious that you should remember my speaking of the hospital, my lord," Dr. Ames said, regaining his crisp tone. "Do you have an interest in children?"

"Children? Why, I suppose I may. I have never found them objectionable but then have never been about any other than my brother's."

Ames's face blanched under the explosion of a fearful new thought as he asked timorously, "You find children of the lower classes repulsive then, my lord?"

Kenton burst into laughter, disconcerting his visitor. "I am sorry, Dr. Ames, but you couldn't have asked that question if you had even once followed me about the combe. When I replied to your question I had in mind living with children. My wife died childless only a brief year after our marriage and so my brief stays at my brother's are my only experience with children in a household." He waved aside the condolences Ames was about to offer. "That was many years past and I am not unhappy.

"As for children—they follow me about like puppies and I do enjoy them. Most I find to be agreeable and eager to please."

Almost clapping his hands, a beaming smile on his face, Dr. Ames scooted to the edge of his chair. His words tumbled over each other in his excitement. "That is what I had hoped to hear, Lord Kenton, for I have a . . . a scheme, Dr. Fowler calls it. In all fairness I must tell you he frowned upon my venturing to ask your aid." Halting as abruptly as he had begun, he sat as if expecting an answer.

"The question, Doctor? What is it you wish from me—a donation for the hospital? I would be happy to . . ."

"Oh, no, Lord Kenton. Pardon me, in my excitement I have become grossly forgetful. The aid I seek does not concern finances—not at least of a monetary sort. It is the old Irwin Manor that is at the eastern edge of your lands that interests me."

"The Irwin Manor? Of what use can it be to you? No one has lived in it since my greataunt passed away several years past," Kenton answered, puzzled.

"But I understand the buildings themselves are in useable form?"

"Yes, I have maintained them in useable condition."

Dr. Ames gulped and ventured courageously onward. "I wish you to give me the use of your buildings and a small plot of ground about them for use as gardens and play areas."

"And who is to make use of this donation?"

"Oh, it will not be a permanent gift, my lord," the young doctor hastened to correct. "Just until I am able to locate something . . . well, something that is perhaps closer to London."

Understanding dawned at last. "You wish to bring ill foundlings here?" Lord Kenton asked with mild surprise. "Do you not think there will be objection from the people of the area?"

Dedication and enthusiasm lined the doctor's bright face. "There would be none brought with a disease harmful to aught but himself. Truly, my lord," he continued earnestly, "if you could see the overcrowded conditions of the hospital, the state of many of the children's health, you would not hesitate for a moment. For many the only chance for life will be the clean, fresh air of the combe and the improved conditions we could offer here." He rose to take his leave. "You need not answer today, my lord. Please do consider it."

"What are your plans for financing such a venture? Even with a roof over them you would have to clothe, feed, and have supervision for the children."

"All that has been considered carefully. Lord Montague, one of the trustees of the Children's Hospital, has agreed to fund the venture for one year providing adequate shelter can be found. Women with suitable backgrounds are known to me who would care for the children and, of course, I had hoped to use local women for the necessary cleaning, washing, and sewing."

"You have this quite well thought out," Kenton noted.

"Does not the success of any venture depend upon that?"

Nodding, Kenton rose.

Ames took his look for one of refusal. "Lord Kenton, I beseech you to think upon this before reaching a decision. The children's plight is truly in the extreme. I could not impinge upon the delicate sensibilities of Lady Joanne with descriptions of their condition but will not hesitate to give such to you."

"That will not be necessary, Dr. Ames," Kenton assured him. "I shall have my agent draw up an agreement for the term of one year—say for a nominal rent of one pound. Would that be satisfactory?"

For a startled instant Ames was motionless. Then half-shouting he bounded the few steps to Kenton's side and began pumping his hand. "Satisfactory? My lord, I am forever in your debt. Any wish of yours I can fulfill will be granted—you need do naught but ask. I must go at once," he said, finally releasing his lordship's hand. "I must send the letters to begin making the arrangements. Please excuse my hasty departure."

"Quite all right, Doctor. You may collect the keys of the manor on the morrow."

"Thank you, my lord. You will not regret your generosity." His half-trot stopped at the study door.

"Please express my regrets to Lady Knoll for not taking my leave of her personally."

Kenton nodded, his eyes following the retreating man's back. Perhaps, he mused to himself, this foundling home will prove a valuable tool in Joanne's education.

Casting about the garden in search of Joanne, Lord Kenton came upon one of the gardeners.

"Have you see the Lady Joanne, Samuel?"

"Aye, milord. The lady was at the east end of the garden," the middle-aged man said, doffing his hat respectfully, "and it did not seem she was set on ending her walk there." He nodded at Lord Kenton's thank you, watched his master's swift stride briefly, and returned to his work. The odd doings of his lordship were not his concern.

Familiar with every blade of grass, shrub, and tree, it did not take Kenton long to realize that the gardener was correct; Joanne was not in the gardens. Samuel would have seen her if she had returned to the manor house, he reasoned, pausing to consider where she could have gone. His head swung in an arch, following the outer borders of the gardens—at this side of the manor the woods had been allowed to remain in their natural state beyond the clipped neatness of the grounds. Rocks, tangled undergrowth, and spidery vines vied with each other beneath the drooping branches of the tall, generations-old trees. A bright patch of flowered cloth caught his eye—a frown wrinkled his brow. So she had ventured off—neither suitably shod nor with a guide. His long strides ended as Kenton entered the woods. Not far in there were further signs of Joanne's direction. Broken branches, moss trampled upon the rocks, vines pulled away from the shrubs, and sagging limbs all told a tale. A rueful smile formed as he dealt with the snagging, grasping branches, weeds, and vines that clutched at his breeches and tore at his coat—Joanne was getting her due for this frolic and showing a degree of tenacity along with her foolhardiness in continuing her jaunt farther than he had expected.

The bright yellow and white of her form appeared to Lord Kenton's left. The lady he sought was seated rather unglamourously upon a rough, moss-covered stone, gingerly trying to inspect the sole of an awkwardly upraised foot.

This foot was dropped quickly as she turned a startled face toward the sounds of a rapidly approaching person. The snapping of twigs beneath his feet echoed like a rampaging beast to the footsore and weary Joanne.

"My lady, if only I had known you desired to see more of the manor's grounds, I would have been delighted to accompany you," Lord Kenton greeted her.

Uncertain disgust played upon Joanne's features as she sought a suitable reply, but the pain in her foot won the battle of concentration.

"Would you care to continue on?" bowed Lord Kenton when no answer was forthcoming.

Stifling the urge to make a face at this constant, repulsively pleasant tormentor, Joanne answered, "I would not inconvenience you, my lord. Dr. Ames should not be left waiting on my account."

"Yes? How pleased I am to hear of your solicitude

for another, but alas it is unnecessary. The good physician has already taken his leave."

Relief and disappointment alternated upon Joanne's features as she rose, carefully putting her weight on her good foot. Why had she expected him to seek her out before the doctor's departure? Her headstrong decision to prove to Kenton she could walk a good deal more than the paltry garden paths had made this unlikely, but that fact mattered not at the moment. Furthermore, she resolved not to be angry—even as she wondered why she should feel angry.

"Dr. Ames did ask me to express his regret at his hurried leavetaking. There was a project he was most eager to set in motion and . . ."

"I do not give a damn! Why should I care what the man is about?" she interrupted heatedly.

"The doctor was certain you would understand his urgency—he has rented Irwin Manor, which is in the combe, to use as a foundling house for ill children from London," Kenton continued calmly. "He said he was looking forward to calling upon you again."

A slow blush came to Joanne's pale cheeks as she dropped her eyes before his steady gaze. Forgetful of why she had paused, she stepped forward.

Kenton grabbed her arm as she gasped and her face contorted in pain. "What is it?" he asked urgently.

"My foot—I must have a thorn lodged it in," she said, grateful for the strong arm to lean upon.

"Sit down," he commanded briskly, helping her step back. With competent quickness he knelt, tossed aside her skirts, and took the injured foot in hand. Slim brown fingers untied the lacing and pulled off the stained, worn satin slipper. Cool hands moved smoothly over the foot; there was a stab of pain. A grunt of satisfaction from Kenton and the offending thorn was removed. "Had I known that you were intent upon wandering off, I would have brought the doctor with me," he noted, tossing the three-quarter-inch-long thorn aside and pressing the injured spot to halt the bleeding.

Hoping to forestall a scolding, Joanne ventured, "He is a strange man."

"Why do you say that?" Kenton asked, looking up.

Joanne shrugged, a contemptuous cast coming over her. "I have met one or two surgeons among my father's friends—not a one ever had less than a bottle before he came to breakfast, and yet this Dr. Ames would not take a single glass of wine."

"Your father took you along on his visits to friends often, then?" Kenton plied gently, returning his eyes to Joanne's foot, his mind attuned only to her answer.

She gave a snort of scornful laughter. "I was never allowed to leave Furness House in all my years before my visit here. No, my father brought his friends there to hunt, I believe, although it appeared to me the wine cellar was more their quarry than any fox or partridge on the estate." An encounter outside the library of Furness House with one of these guests came to mind as she dwelt on those times and Joanne felt her stomach sicken. She stiffened as she remembered the man's drunken, clutching hands.

The tensed muscles caused Kenton to glance up. A scream would not have taken him by surprise, so intense was the shadow of terror and loathing upon her.

"I believe no damage has been done," he said loudly. "I will bind it with this clean kerchief I happened to fetch since I had need of a fresh one," he joked lightly.

"Need of?" Joanne said, her features clearing as the reassuring voice helped her push the memory away.

"Yes . . . you do not recall? I had to remove some wine from . . . odd how it did not remain in its glass," Kenton teased tossing her a warm smile. "There." He pulled the slipper back into place. "Take my arm and we will make our way back to the manor house slowly. Tomorrow I shall show you a more suitable walking path and we shall have some proper walking shoes made for you—no more of this."

The usual half-angry, disgusted frown appeared at his words and he smiled wider, causing her frown to deepen in return. As they made their way, he chatted lightly, trying to amuse and distract her from whatever had frightened her—that instance firming his determination to learn more of her childhood.

Joanne's thoughts had gone back to the too-near past. Hatred and bitterness were deeply rooted and now they welled up within. Any of the gentler thoughts she had had and felt were wiped out. Kenton was the focus of her pent-up disillusionment—he was the only target close at hand—the only one she could focus those feelings on.

I hate him, I hate him, she thought over and over. *There is no difference—not at Furness House—not here. What will become of me?*

Chapter Nine

The Billingsgate language coming from the kitchen directed Lord Kenton to his destination. Mrs. Caern, her face outraged, stood barring Lady Joanne's entry into the food-filled pantry with an upraised rolling pin.

Hearing his steps, Joanne whirled to face him. "You have no right to starve me. Tell that old harridan to step aside," she demanded angrily.

"Or what?" his lordship asked, leaning lazily against a work counter.

"She has threatened me—says she will hit me with that . . . that club," Joanne protested, waving a hand at the weapon.

"Ordinarily I do not approve of violence," Kenton spoke easily. "But the kitchen is Mrs. Caern's domain," he added, seeing umbrage flame to his housekeepeer's face. "And as such, she rules it as she sees fit."

"But she will not obey my orders or let me pass." Indignation had brought a livid red to Joanne's features.

"Thus you must learn that no one ever has everything they desire," he told her, the same seriousness filling his voice as it had done whenever a point was being made in their many confrontations since her arrival.

"You can't do this," Joanne screamed and stomped her foot while casting about for something to throw.

"But I am doing nothing, my lady." Kenton feigned puzzlement at her ire, while assessing the situation. That it had reached a physical confrontation called for a desperate solution. He had forbade his household to react to Joanne; perhaps the time had come to change that. "Since you are having such a *pleasant* discussion with Mrs. Caern, I shall leave you to complete it. My compliments," he nodded to his housekeeper. With a smile to Lady Joanne he walked leisurely from the kitchen. A large crock smashed to pieces against the door's frame as he passed through it, apparently oblivious to the shower of fragments.

"That . . . that beast of a man. Of all the foul . . ."

"Watch your words, milady." Mrs. Caern advanced threateningly. "This is enough! Lord Jason should have sent ye off to London the day ye came. Ye've done nothing but despoil his house, scream, and thrash at everyone who tries to help ye and made each meal a battleground this whole month past, what with yer coarse ways and foul mouth. I'll not have it any longer." Slowly the rolling pin was lowered, her anger spent. The old woman's shoulders sagged tiredly. "Haven't ye any change of heart? Haven't ye seen yer reflection of late, milady—seen the improvement? Ye've the makin's of a comely maid but fer yer sharp tongue and unruly temper."

This sudden change in Mrs. Caern's tact pricked the bubble of anger surrounding Joanne. Confusion rushed into its place. "What?" she questioned as tears welled in her eyes. Anger, hatred, resentment she could battle with relish; this sudden concern—kindness—routed her, and she fled.

"Lord preserve us," Mrs. Caern muttered in relief. "What will become of this?"

Safe in her chamber, Joanne flung herself upon her bed. Her bile, her one protection, had deserted her. Its companion, fear, now came to the fore, What if Lord Kenton decided to return her to her father? "Then I'd be free of his high and mighty lordship—free of this place," she snorted, looking about the barren chamber, its emptiness an indictment of her unrepenting hostility. *How have I managed this long?* she wondered, and the incident which had brought about the minor truce that had held till this morn flashed vividly to mind.

Lord Kenton had at first been lenient—his calm voice and relaxed manner oblivious to the outrages Joanne perpetrated upon his staff and himself as well as his manor. The second week of her stay saw a tightening of his discipline, especially in regard to her ladyship's atrocious dining habits.

On this particular eve a dish at a time had been ordered taken from the table as he noted her dislike of each (the lady being inclined to forgo the use of her utensils and grab at the food). Only the platter of beef had remained and she had made a lunging grab, securing most of the beef in her lap. Not only had he taken this from her but decreed that henceforth she would be served a prepared plate. The next morn the decree was tested.

Sitting to breakfast, Lord Kenton maintained a stream of pleasantries as he was served a platter of kidney pie, cold pheasant, and warm biscuits dripping with butter. Lady Joanne querulously ignored him, vulgarly demanding her food be brought. Her eyes brightened at sight of Nell coming into the dining room. His lordship decided it was time for her first true lesson.

"Nell, take that tray back to the kitchen. I cannot have Lady Knoll's sensibilities disturbed so early in the morn by such a coarse breakfast. Some thin porridge, please," he ordered. "Are you of good appetite this morn, my lady?" he asked, savouring a piece of pheasant.

Lady Joanne stared at him incredulously. Wrath grew to explosive proportions as she awaited Nell's return. The serving maid returned reluctantly and gingerly placed the bowl before her ladyship, retreating as soon as the deed was done. Wordlessly Lady Joanne looked across the table at her tormentor. A gleam came to her eye and her tightly compressed lips eased into the hint of glee. Picking up the bowl, she flung the contents across the table into Lord Kenton's face, bursting into laughter as the warm milk-laced gruel dripped from his visage and joined the remainder splattered across his jabot and frock coat.

Calmly Lord Kenton dabbed at his face, and called for Nell.

The young serving girl gasped at the sight his lordship presented and looked aghast at Lady Joanne's mocking laughter.

"Please bring another bowl of porridge," Kenton told her. "There has been a minor accident with the first."

"Shouldn't I first . . . I mean, milord, you . . ." Words ended as Kenton's expression hardened. "As you wish, milord," Nell swallowed and hurried to do as told. In a thrice she returned.

"Bring it to me," Kenton commanded as she hesitated before the table. "You may go. Close the doors."

"Do you mean to improve your appearance further?" sneered Lady Joanne. A shocked gasp came from her as the contents of the bowl he held hit her full in the face.

"I did not find it a particularly pleasurable experience, myself," he quietly noted. "Do not do it to someone else if you don't want it done to yourself." He rose. "I shall see you at lunch."

So began our uneasy truce, she thought. *At least I learned not to confront him. And your behaviour toward Mrs. Caern? Nell, Meg, and the others?*

"They are servants," she spoke aloud, hitting the bed pillow roughly. "They do not matter." Her words ended unconvincingly. *And they have never been unkind,* her conscience added.

Indeed, the country openness of the serving maids—their happy spirits and unhesitant kindness—had had an effect on Lady Joanne despite herself. She found it increasingly difficult to enjoy her tantrums, even when they were successful. Frightening and insulting others, she learned, held little satisfaction when like feelings were not returned. Her language slowly began to improve—out of his lordship's hearing. Her manners were similarly affected—out of his lordship's presence.

Petulantly Joanne admitted to herself that this morn's outburst against Mrs. Caern was not caused by the overwhelming desire to eat but by the overpowering need to press some reaction from Lord Kenton. His ever-enduring calm was irritating, infuriating. But worse, she could not fathom why it disquieted her so.

A knock on her door interrupted her reverie.

"His lordship is wantin' ye to come to the library, milady," Meg announced, hesitant to enter, for one never knew what type of response would come. "Lord Kenton asks ye to come right away," she added when Joanne didn't move.

"I will," Joanne answered hollowly, certain she was going to be asked to leave Kentoncombe. *Oh, Lord,* she thought as slow steps took her toward the library, *let me remain a little longer. I will do better. I will die if I must return to Furness House.* She shuddered, then stiffened herself. Lord Kenton must never know she wished to stay. That satisfaction would never be his.

Lord Jason was totally immersed in the problem of Lady Joanne. The hope that the atmosphere of Kentoncombe, that the good-hearted treatment and example of those surrounding her ladyship would gentle her ways, appeared frustratingly hopeless in light of this morn's incident. At least they did not come to actual blows, he smiled wryly. *Poor Mrs. Caern—I must do something to make up for what she has endured of late.* What kept him from abandoning this uncivilized termagant? He dared not probe why.

"Well?" Lady Joanne demanded, closing the doors behind her.

"I have decided . . ." Kenton began and noticed Joanne pale slightly. What did she expect? "That it would be best if you were to . . ." he paused wondering again at the play of emotion he saw on her features. "That it would be best if you were to visit Irwin Manor a few days a week and visit with the children. Dr. Ames tells me five are expected any day and that there would be no danger to your health. It is the sort of thing you should be doing in your position in society." He turned to the windows, disturbed by her lack of response. "I have tried to explain that certain qualities are expected of a lady. It is all very well that you can read the classics in their original text, that your grasp of the sciences is remarkable. But these accomplishments are frowned upon by society. Madame de Genlis, in her book on educated young ladies, goes so far as to say that they 'render women singularly unsuitable for domestique life.' Women are expected to . . ."

The words became an indistinguishable babble as Kenton continued. A surge of joy more powerful than any hate she had ever experienced filled Joanne. She was to stay.

Chapter Ten

"Mrs. Caern?" Lady Joanne approached the elderly housekeeper nervously.

"Aye, milady," she answered, marveling again at the change in her ladyship since she had been going to Irwin Manor. The three weeks since the visits had begun had seen a definite improvement. Outbursts of temper still occurred, but they were no longer daily and her ladyship had even consented to letting Lord Jason instruct her in the arts of society in their hours after supping.

"I was wondering . . . that is . . ." Lady Joanne stumbled. Having never done other than demand and bully, she found her present course very difficult.

Seeing her distress, the good housekeeper rose to her aid. "Do you need help with what's in the basket?" she asked kindly.

Lady Joanne nodded. "Mrs. Brasmen—the head matron at Irwin Manor . . . well, there was this mending that needed to be done and she carried on so about what fine stitches *ladies* have that before I knew it I had offered to take care of it." Despair tinged Joanne's features.

"And you don't know how to?" guessed Mrs. Caern. "Why, milady, that's easily solved. Come, I'll fetch me needles and thread and soon ye'll have the right of it."

"You . . . you will help me?"

" 'Tis no reason not to," Mrs. Caern shrugged.

Thankfulness pressed Joanne to reach out and hug the woman but hate and distrust had not been entirely washed away. She held herself back, giving a wondering smile instead.

"How did you find the children at Irwin today?" Lord Kenton asked Joanne at supper.

"Four more arrived today," she answered. "Dr. Ames said he expects a score more within the next two months. I think I shall begin going to Irwin an additional day," she added, keeping her eyes on her plate. For the first time since her arrival she was thankful that eating was to be done mainly with the right hand, for the fingers of the left were painfully pricked and reddened from her lesson in needlework. Their condition was far worse than necessary, for Mrs. Caern had cautioned her to stop, but Joanne had proven as dogged in mending as she had been unrelenting in her hostility. Her worst fear now was that Lord Kenton would laugh if he saw her hand or the mending she had done. Although wretched by Mrs. Caern's standard, it was a source of great pride to Joanne.

"I am happy to see that you are beginning to enjoy your visit here," Kenton said smiling. "Now let us see if you recall the proper forms of address. Begin with that of squire."

The meal passed quickly—Lord Kenton and Lady Joanne coming to words only once this eve.

"I see little difference in a marquess and a duke, especially if he is not a royal duke," she snapped after being corrected upon their address. "Why should one be merely 'my lord' and the other 'your grace'? It is ridiculous." She threw her fork to the table.

"A lady never drops her silver," Kenton admonished. "And the Duke of Newcastle would certainly wish to be addressed as your grace."

"I'll drop what I wish." Her temper flared at his further correction. "And since it is highly unlikely I shall ever meet the duke, he may keep his grace and your grace, my lord." She waved her left hand angrily, dismissing the subject.

Kenton saw the reddened, sore fingers at once. "Your hand," he demanded. "What has happened to it?" Concern darkened his brow.

Blinking back angry tears at being discovered, Joanne said, "Learning needlework, damn you." Pushing back her chair, she ran from the room.

Staring after her, Kenton frowned. His plans had progressed far better than he could have hoped. The children at Irwin Manor had taken Joanne's mind from herself and allowed her to expend her energies and expand her emotional field. She had even smiled a time or two in the last weeks. They had developed a battling camaraderie in her lessons. *So why did she not tell me about this?* he wondered. Refusing to admit that it bothered him, he turned his mind to Mrs.

Caern. I must give her a scold—there is no reason Lady Joanne must scar herself in this pursuit.

September brought the last of summer heat, and hints of autumn coolness were begun to be felt.

"Today a young girl, hardly more than a babe she seems, was brought to Irwin," Lady Joanne told Lord Jason as they walked toward the large parlour in Kentoncombe one evening. "Dr. Ames said she had been at Children's Hospital for over eight months."

"Is she another orphan?"

Lady Joanne shook her head. "He said they believe she is not, but that it cannot be proven. She was found in a basket placed on the hospital's steps one night. A common occurrence, Dr. Ames says. Unwanted." The last word came without thought. Hearing it aloud, Joanne realized she had been drawn to Ellen as much by her own feelings of rejection as by pity for the child. For the first time a glimmer of understanding at her own behaviour dawned.

"Is that all they know of her?" Jason asked a second time, his gaze locked on Joanne's face, wreathed in a softness he had not before seen upon it.

"What? Oh, yes, I believe so. Dr. Ames says there is little hope of learning more. She's just a tiny thing with the largest blue eyes I have ever seen and the palest blond hair. When you look at her, she is so thin it seems she must disappear. I held her and rocked her for some time this afternoon. She seemed so fearful, I had to do something to comfort her. All she did was stare at me."

"She didn't speak? Not even to ask for a sweet?" He thought of his own visits at Irwin with a smile.

"The papers that came with her state that she has never spoken—not since she was found on the hospital's steps. Dr. Ames said he hoped it is merely caused by her poor health and her fear at being in the hospital—but that she may be dumb."

"Is she deaf also?" Kenton asked, opening the parlor doors.

"No." A huge smile came to Joanne's lips. "I sang her a song Mrs. Caern had taught me and she went right to sleep."

"She may have just been exhausted from the journey," Lord Jason said gently.

"No, I am certain she heard me. Dr. Ames agreed," Joanne insisted. "But why have we come to this parlour?" She looked about the spacious chamber. The furniture had been moved to one side and the carpet rolled up.

Ignoring the irritation caused by the oft-repeated Dr. Ames Kenton smiled and made a leg. "This eve, my lady, you shall learn the minuet. Though to be honest," his smile twisted, "my prowess as dance master will leave much to be desired. It has been years . . ."

"Dancing? I have no need of it," Joanne objected.

"It is essential for a lady." His look brooked no argument.

After an hour of awkward attempt and at times farcical rehearsal Kenton called for Mrs. Caern to bring refreshments. "Let us sit," he told Joanne. "You have earned a rest."

"When shall you see that this is impossible?" Joanne shook her head as she sat beside him on the overstuffed sofa, an acquisition of Kenton's last visit to

London from Chippendale's shop in St. Martin's Lane.

"Do not be discouraged. You have a fair degree of natural grace," he returned without the usual bantering tones. "Thank you, Mrs. Caern," he told the housekeeper as she set the tray of wine upon the slab table near them. "Will you fetch the magazine that arrived in today's post—it is in my study." Turning to Joanne, he told her, "I have decided that it is essential you see how ladies of fashion dress and deport themselves and so I have subscribed to *The Ladies Magazine*." He rose and served Joanne, taking his seat as Mrs. Caern returned. "Ah, yes. Now let me see." He paged slowly. "Here it is. This is how the fashionable miss is gowned. By comparison your hair is abominably dressed and your gown sadly lacking in hoops, hip pads, and furbelows."

"What is wrong with my hair?" she demanded, still overly sensitive of her shorn locks, even though her hair had finally grown enough to be pinned.

"The proper toilet for a ridotto demands your hair be dressed to at least fifteen inches in height—see our young miss here. Hair pads aid this I am told or more simply, a periwig is used. Some, I am told, reach immense proportions. Naturally this 'masterpiece' is powdered and bedecked with all manner of fustian. The young lady here seems to fancy feathers and jewels for hers."

Joanne eyed the sketch skeptically.

"Even the men," Kenton continued, "do not remain unaffected. "When I was last in London I was given an advertisement which recommended tye wigs, long bobs, cleric bobs, and even spensers. A true gentleman of fashion has his head shorn for the wearing of these majestic creations," he laughed.

She shook her head in disbelief, taking in his own attractive dark hair, neatly dressed in a queue held by a black ribbon.

"It is only because I am not fashionable and because country life allows informality that I have spurned the peruke. Once you go to London you will be so dressed the majority of the time. But enough of this." He closed the magazine and rose. Offering his hand to Joanne, he assisted, her, gazing at her features as if seeing them for the first time. *She is comely,* he thought.

"Is my hair truly displeasing?" Joanne asked as they assumed the opening stance of the minuet.

"No, my lady," he assured her, making a leg as she curtsied. "It is . . . suitable." He took her hand, their arms brushing as they turned into the first movement. Kenton felt suddenly mesmerized as they moved through the dance. At the end he stood holding her hand, a sudden realization dawning.

Joanne became puzzled by the strange look that came to Lord Kenton's features as he looked at her. "Have I done it wrongly?" she asked.

"No." Kenton dropped her hand. "There will be no more lessons this eve," he said gruffly. "Good eve." Turning on his heel he was gone.

Chapter Eleven

" 'Tis a great change," Nell said to Ann as the two worked diligently at polishing the dark oak paneling and the massive furniture of the dining hall at Kentoncombe.

"Aye, one'd never know her ladyship for the same person. 'Haps the cooler weather of October has done it?" Ann speculated as she paused in her efforts on the planked table. "Or that young Dr. Ames—he could be the cause."

"That's a far more likely reason," laughed Nell. "If he's not here, it seems she's fetchin' things to Irwin for the foundlings."

"An' ignorin' his lordship all the while. He's just as much the gentleman as can be no matter what she does or says."

"Me mum says it's just his lordship's way—to help those who need it . . ."

"Why are you two chattering?" Mrs. Caern's annoyed voice asked. She came into the room seconds later to find both girls vigourously rubbing beeswax and oil into a luxurious shine. "See to it you finish

in an hour. There's much more to be done this day."
The elderly housekeeper stayed a few moments to ensure continued zeal and considered scolding the girls
for what she had overheard. Both were young and
had been at the manor less than a year, however. During that time they had shown good natures and were
hardworking and Mrs. Caern was certain the gossip
was harmless. As she herself stood in wonder of the
change in Lady Joanne in the months since her coming to Kentoncombe, she decided to forgo the reprimand.

Anyone seeing her ladyship now would marvel. No
longer ponderously heavy but with only a healthy excess, her nature had changed as drastically as her
frame. Just as the chopped hair now fell in shimmer-
ing brown waves about the thinning oval face with
its high cheekbones and aristocratic nose, the eyes now
laughed and the lips smiled. Pleasantries came forth
more often than insults and commands. In fact, the
young woman could be seen to be a caring person
when it came to her efforts with the foundlings,
thought Mrs. Caern.

This point only increased the bewilderment of her
behaviour toward Lord Kenton. While Lady Joanne's
manner toward all in the combe had gradually evolved
into the well-behaved and genteel, she reverted when
it came to her dealings with his lordship. It almost appeared that the two enjoyed their encounters, but
Mrs. Caern knew all was not well. In her position
as housekeeper for over one and forty years she had
known Lord Jason from birth. Coming across him
after passing Lady Joanne outside the library doors
some two weeks ago, she was taken aback by the look

of deep sorrow furrowing his brow. Such a look she had not seen upon him since the early mourning days after Lady Kenton's death.

"Milord, is there something I can do?" she asked in her concern.

Slowly his eyes focused upon her and a sad smile struggled for a hold upon his lips. "No, Mrs. Caern—there is nothing." He started to turn away, then swung back. "Yes, there is something I would like you to see to. Summon the best seamstress there is to be found in Ilfracombe. Lady Joanne's wardrobe must be improved upon. Instruct the woman to bring only bright colors and patterns suitable to a young lady and have made some new day dresses and some suitable for evening wear.

"If Lady Joanne objects, tell her that her father left instructions to have her clothing added to periodically as was needed and that you see the need. When the new garments are finished, give the old ones to the seamstress to be given to some poor deserving woman in Ilfracombe. Under no circumstances am I to be mentioned—do you understand this?"

"Wouldn't it be best for her ladyship to know . . ."

"Deny any involvement on my part," Lord Kenton interrupted adamantly. "I must see to some business. Have the seamstress send her bills to me. Tell her they will be taken care of upon completion of the gowns."

"Aye, milord," Mrs. Caern answered, frowning. "But there will be more than outer garments needed."

Lord Kenton stared momentarily, then broke into a smile at Mrs. Caern's discomfiture. "See to whatever is needed."

"Aye, milord." Setting about the task, Mrs. Caern

thought, first Lord Jason is in the depths of sadness, then bright as a schoolboy as he orders gowns and yet refuses to take credit for the deed—what was in his mind? She was uncertain, but her motherly instinct gave her an idea she did not like.

The new dresses and gowns had come as a spirit-brightening surprise for Joanne.

"My father left directions I was to have them?" she asked the housekeeper repeatedly.

Gritting her teeth, Mrs. Caern assured the girl over and over this was so and marveled bitterly as Lady Joanne became even colder toward Lord Jason.

A heavy sigh came from the white-haired house-keeper's ample bosom as she watched the young girls polishing so steadily under her gaze. "Hurry now," she told them. "There is much to be done before the supper party tonight." She headed back to the kitchen to check with the cook once more.

This was to be the largest and most formal dinner in years at Kentoncombe and no detail was to be left unattended. Mrs. Caern shook her head, for no matter what was said she knew the dinner was being given so that Lady Joanne could practice all the skills Lord Jason had been so patiently instilling in her all this time. Humphing, she thought: *Probably just so she can be a fancy lady in London.* She halted abruptly. "Why, aye," she said aloud, "the girl has to be leaving—in less than six months is the new season they speak about in London." Her steps went more slowly now in the cook's direction as she realized that somehow it had seemed that Lady Joanne would always be at Kentoncombe.

* * *

A late-morning fall shower had left puddles strewn across the road Lady Joanne was gingerly walking. At the sound of a carriage pulled by a single horse she glanced back.

Dr. Ames smiled broadly as he drew the gig to a halt at her side. "Would you honor me with your presence, Lady Knoll?" he asked. "I believe I know your direction."

"You and your gig are a welcome sight, Doctor," Joanne answered welcomingly. "The rains will make a mire of this road and everything else if they continue. No, do not step down. Take the basket and I can manage." Freed of its weight, she lifted her skirts and took Ames's hand to steady herself as she stepped up and sat in the hooded gig.

"Surely you have not already completed the sewing you took with you on your last visit to Irwin?" Dr. Ames asked, glancing down at the neatly folded children's garments in the basket between them.

"There was little to do and I enjoy it immensely." She blushed modestly. "Mrs. Caern says I have learned to ply a needle with skill. I have her word the work is well done," she ended, proud of her newly acquired skill.

"I am certain it is," the young physician said in return. "You have been a great help since the beginning and now with the children you are becoming indispensable. It does puzzle me though, why you trouble so over my little foundlings."

"There is no mystery in that. I too was a foundling . . ." she paused as he glanced at her questioningly. "But most of all it is the first time in my life that I feel useful—wanted, needed perhaps. The children are so willing to give of what little they have—be it only love. Tell me, do you still have hope Ellen will speak?"

"Her physical health has much improved since she came to Irwin—due in large part to your care," he smiled. "At times I wonder if she is not older than the four years we believe her to be. There is a sense of wisdom about her."

"Yes, she looks like a sad old woman at times as she sits watching the other children play," Joanne agreed.

"I fear her lack of response to others is a sign her mind may have been affected—by disease or misuse," Dr. Ames noted sadly. "Perhaps that is why she does not speak. If so, she may never."

"Oh, I hope not," Joanne said alarmed. "Mrs. Caern helped me make this rag doll," she said, reaching into the basket and drawing out a floppy creature dressed in scraps from her own new day dresses from beneath the stack of clothing. "Do you think this will please Ellen?"

"What gift from you would not be pleasing, my lady?" he answered, taking his eyes from the road to gaze tenderly at Joanne.

In her naiveté she laughed. "You say the oddest things, Dr. Ames. Seriously, I do hope she will like it— I know I would have."

A crooked smile had found its way to Dr. Ames's face—caused by her first remark, it was lengthened by the second. The daughter of an earl would have been pleased by a rag doll? Shaking his head, he flicked the reins, hurrying the horse onward. *What strange comments from this ever prettier Lady Knoll,* he thought.

"Where can she be?" Lord Kenton asked for what sounded like the thousandth time.

"I do not know, milord," Mrs. Caern repeated. "She went out right after luncheon to take the sewing she had done back to Irwin Manor. I understood she was to return immediately after delivering it. Perhaps she stayed on a bit to visit with the new little girl, Ellen. She is quite taken with the child. Why, she even had me help her make a rag doll for her." A smile appeared as she thought of Lady Joanne's eagerness over a simple doll.

"It will be dusk soon and rain may be coming in," continued the paternal rumblings from his lordship.

" 'Tis probably the doctor, Lord Jason," said Mrs. Caern. "If he is at Irwin he may have insisted Lady Joanne wait until he is finished so he can drive her home. After all, it is several hours before the guests are to arrive."

"I will wait only a half hour more—tell me if she has not come home by then," he instructed, worry creasing his usually tranquil features.

"Do not concern yourself overly—she is excited about the party and would not wish to be late," Mrs. Caern assured Kenton.

An unconvinced shake of his head answered her. Something was not right—he could feel it. "I will be in my study."

Seated at his desk, Lord Kenton watched the low clouds tumbling slowly, ever-increasing signs that rain soon would be falling. Abstractedly he drummed his fingers upon the desk top, then unlocked and pulled open the center drawer.

A smile replaced the frown as he removed a small, delicately carved oak jewel box. Unlatching the clasp, he gazed down at the simple golden rose nestled in the red velvet, its small gold chain draped across the smooth folds. Kenton's smile deepened as he thought what Joanne's reaction to the coat-of-arms chamber would be this eve. Over the past three months he had slowly ordered the return of various items of its decorations and adornments. This day he had seen the armorial shields and swords hung back in their places along the bare wall and the replacement of his family crest and the mirrored sconces. The rose so fragilely formed from gold which lay before him was modeled after the one found in his crest and repeated in the Elizabethan frieze about the chamber that Joanne had once remarked upon. Knowing she had no jewelry, Lord Kenton had had the rose wrought for her—it would be the perfect complement to the simple blue gown she would wear this eve. Not even to himself would he admit how much he hoped she would be pleased by the gift.

"Milord! Milord!" rang into the study. The carved jewel box was snapped shut, replaced in the drawer, and the lock turned.

Mrs. Caern stumbled and righted herself as she hurried in, ashen. "Milord, Dr. Ames is without—he says he just left Irwin and Lady Joanne was not there—nor to be seen on the road."

There was a pause as confirmation of his fears settled in Kenton's mind. The steely calmness of his ways asserted itself. "Is Dr. Ames still here?" he asked quietly.

"Aye, milord. He said he would await you."

"Fetch my cloak and gloves. Send one of the maids to order Asteron saddled and brought to the doors at once." Patting her on her broad back he told her, "Remain calm, now." They entered the corridor and went their separate ways.

Pointed questions to and quick answers from Dr. Ames put no light on Joanne's whereabouts. The doctor had taken her to Irwin but was certain she had taken her leave at least two hours earlier than he because of the dinner party. While the two men discussed the possibilities, Mrs. Caern appeared with the cloak and gloves. The warmth of the cloak when he swung it about his shoulders heightened Kenton's concern. The evening chill could be harmful to one not dressed properly.

Two men came from the stables—one leading Asteron.

"Ben," Lord Kenton called to the second, "fetch me a lantern." His attention swinging back to the doctor he reiterated, "We are agreed then. You shall go back to Irwin and search there. I will search along the road and the paths she may have taken."

With a farewell nod Dr. Ames whipped his horse; the gig lurched forward as he set a swift pace up the hill.

At the door of Kentoncombe, his lordship swung into the saddle and took the lantern. "Ben, take three men—mount yourselves and search along the main road to Irwin—Lady Knoll has not returned. I will search the footpaths she may have taken. If you find her, take her to the closest manor house and send word to the other." He started forward but swung Asteron back in a circle to the doorway. "Send messages to those invited to the dinner stating it will be held at a later date—with my apologies," he shouted to Mrs. Caern. Digging his heels into Asteron's flanks, he surged forward to the hilltop and was gone.

The last glimmering rays of the sun, shrouded by clouds. Full darkness hovered on the day's edge as Kenton galloped onward. Asteron was drawn to a halt as Kenton paused to consider which path to take first and lit the lantern. Holding the flickering beam aloft, he urged Asteron to a brisk walk. If Joanne were along either path he could only hope she would see the light or hear him call and shout out in answer. If she were unconscious, it would be full light before they could find her. His heart tightened at the thought—she could catch a death of a chill or . . . Kenton stopped the wild racing of his imnd and peered more steadily into the milky fog slowly engulfing everything.

Joanne would be found—found unharmed and probably up to one of her headstrong impulses, he told himself, attempting to find some humour in the situation. But, by God, she would be found, for she had long ago ceased to be a stranger, a mere challenge to his skill. She was more. Yes, she was more, he realized; his heart knew how much more.

Chapter Twelve

Rain pattered lightly upon the dusty, smeared window of the attic chamber. Huddled in one of its dusty, web-filled corners, Joanne hugged her knees tightly to her chest as the rain began drumming on the roof, the sound filling the darkness. Terror drove all thought away.

Tiny feet scratched and scurried across the room. Joanne bolted upright, a terrified statue, then ran to the wall before her, feeling frantically for the door. It would not budge as it had not done since the bar on the outside had crashed down with such thunderous finality several hours ago. She had cried for help till her voice was a raspy, useless thread. *I shall go mad,* she thought, sagging against the door, *utterly mad.*

You never did when that witch of a nanny locked you in as a child and you won't now, her mind heckled her.

"I don't want to think of it," Joanne cried in a painful croak, despair drawing nearer. "Please, I don't want to think."

* * *

"Are you certain there was no sign of her?" Lord Kenton shouted at Ben through the blustering wind and squalls of rain.

"Aye, milord. Nothin' can be seen. We must wait till break o' day to search," the groom shouted.

"Look. Someone be comin'," another groom yelled.

All heads turned to the bobbing light coming from the direction of Irwin Manor. Kenton raised his cloak to allow the light of his shielded lantern to shine and the bobbing slowed. The men on the road moved to one side as the gig halted in their midst.

"Did you find her?" Dr. Ames called to Kenton.

Sidling Asteron to the gig's side, his lordship shook his head. "What did you learn?"

"Not much. The head matron said she saw Lady Knoll walking about the manor with Ellen. Miss Hampsen said she thought it odd Lady Knoll did not bid farewell, but Ellen was abed and she decided her ladyship was in a hurry on this occasion."

"Did anyone see her leave Irwin?" Kenton asked.

"No, none saw her even on the grounds. We have searched all the buildings several times over."

"The girl, Ellen. Did you question her?"

"The child? The matron said she was unusually upset and refused to eat, so I did not think it wise. There could be little learned, for she has yet to speak a word."

"I will see that for myself," Kenton flung back. Handing the lantern to another, he urged Asteron toward Irwin at the fastest pace he dared in the treacherous muddy footing. The others followed.

Dr. Ames cursed, startling himself. It was impossible to turn the gig here. Flicking the reins angrily, he mumbled, "Kenton is mad to think Lady Joanne is still at Irwin. The fool—why does he not search the paths. I would . . ." his voice died away. There was naught he could do but make for the junction so he could return to Irwin.

Mud splashed onto Lord Kenton was washed away by the rain squalls as he galloped on the waterlogged road to Irwin. His usual concern for his steed was forgotten in his urgency to find Joanne.

When Ben and the other grooms sloshed up the steps of Irwin shivering in their drenched clothing, their discomfort was forgotten as they heard a very unfamiliar sound—their master's upraised voice.

"Quiet all of you," Kenton roared at the babbling women surrounding him.

The matron and her underlings were startled into instant silence and drew together protectively.

Mrs. Brasmen, chosen as matron because of her size and voice as well as her skill, put her hands on her hips. "I say again that you cannot see the child, my lord. There is nothing she can tell you—she does not speak." The woman paused, then tried another tactic. "Let us dry your cloak," her voice eased its tone, "and make some hot drink to warm you."

During this exchange Ben and his men edged inside the open door, seeking shelter. The dripping of water into a pool about them and the shuffling of their feet as they tried to buff some feeling into the cold numbness drew Kenton's attention. His stance relaxed. "You are correct, Mrs. Brasmen. It would not be of any value to frighten the child." He drew his soaked cloak from his shoulders and held it out. "I would appreciate your taking my men to the kitchen to dry themselves. For myself, some hot chocolate, please."

His calm voice and aristocratic manner stayed Mrs. Brasmen's objections. She had not counted upon a host of wet grooms in her kitchen. "Miss Hampsen, have these men follow you. Instruct Cook to make hot chocolate. Bring it to the library please."

"Be seated, my lord," the matron continued after they reached the library.

"As soon as the chocolate is brought I wish to see the child," Kenton renewed his demand. His look halted her objection. "I do not intend her any harm."

Mrs. Brasmen's jaw worked but she did not speak. Who was she to prevent his lordship in this? It was his generosity that provided the manor house. Summoning her most severe look, she spoke. "As you wish, my lord, but I take no responsibility for the consequences."

Small white feet peeked out from beneath the floor-length bedgown. Ellen's small head hung and her small hand clutched a rag doll as she stood before Lord Kenton.

"Leave us," he instructed the matron. "Come closer, Ellen," he spoke softly. "I have some hot chocolate— would you not like a sip?"

The small head nodded.

"Then come," Kenton urged gently. Like a toy, he lifted Ellen to his lap. Taking his cup he lifted it to the child's lips. Her eyes never left his as she took a sip. "What a pretty doll you have," he admired. "Is this the one Lady Joanne made for you?"

The arms tightened about it; fear came to the wide blue eyes and the bottom lip quivered.

"Lady Joanne gave it to you today, didn't she?" he asked.

Guilt mingled with fear upon Ellen's face.

"Did Lady Joanne leave Irwin today?"

Ellen shook her head.

Lord Kenton was silent for a time, studying the little girl Joanne cared for so much. "Is Lady Joanne still in the Manor?" he asked.

Assured by his soothing voice and calm manner Ellen nodded.

"Could you show me where? Remain here," Kenton instructed Mrs. Brasmen and Miss Hampsen as he followed Ellen into the corridor.

Fear nibbled through Joanne's thin veneer of courage. She snatched at thoughts to hold complete terror at bay. To her surprise her pleasant memories were connected with Lord Kenton. His smiling face and calm voice appeared as clearly as a portrait in her mind's eye. Unconsciously she let down the barrier between them that she had constructed so tenaciously.

He always treats me with respect, she thought. The sound of his "my lady" echoed faintly in her mind and Joanne's smile grew as she recalled the slight inflection he used in those two small words when she was at her most unladylike.

The ragged lightning jarred the darkness. As it slashed through the night, a new thought was revealed.

"Why, I never hated Lord Jason," she marveled aloud. "I never thought . . . I must . . . no. No, it is that he is a father to me." *Yes,* she assured herself silently. *It is just that he is more a father than my own ever was. Will I ever be able to let him know . . .*

"Joanne! Joanne!"

She shook her head—her imagination was becoming too vivid.

"Joanne! Answer me, Joanne!"

Footsteps and a feeble flash of light beneath the door's edge sent her racing to the door. "Jason!" she cried pummeling the door. "You found me," she sobbed with relief as she flew to his arms, clutching him to assure herself of his reality.

"Ellen led me to you," he said softly as his arms closed possessively about her and he savoured the sound of his name upon her lips. "I have found you," he murmured as he laid a kiss upon her tresses, acknowledging his tumultuous feelings.

Neither heard Dr. Ames's call as they stood locked together, Lady Joanne naively certain of her feelings, Jason Kenton reveling in and yet damning his own.

Chapter Thirteen

The bobbing light and excited babble broke the mood enveloping Lady Joanne and Lord Kenton.

"You are unharmed?" he asked, stepping back but keeping his hold upon her.

"I shall always be so with you near," Joanne answered and wondered at the strained look he gave her.

"Thank God!" rang from the far end of the corridor. "You have found her," Dr. Ames exclaimed as his running steps brought him to their side.

Behind him Mrs. Brasmen and Miss Hampsen followed. The matron's keen eye took in Lord Kenton's hold upon Lady Knoll and the young woman's adoring eyes. "A fine business," she muttered, "getting herself lost on purpose." More loudly she exclaimed, "Lady Knoll, oh, the wonder of it. You are found and unharmed. Why, I should have been hysterical ages ago and here you stand so calmly. Surely you must need rest. Come to my chamber—here, I have my vinaigrette." She forced Kenton to step back as she put an arm around Lady Joanne's waist.

"Let me help you," Miss Hampsen added solicitously, looking somewhat enviously from Lord Kenton to Lady Knoll.

Neither lady's movements were misunderstood by the two men. Ames subdued a grin at the sudden awkwardness and Kenton tightened his jaw.

"No, no," laughed Joanne, shrugging free from the two attentive ladies. "I am fine now that I am free," and shared the double meaning with Kenton. Turning to where Ellen stood beside the lamp, Joanne scooped her into her arms. The little girl responded with a choking hug.

The sight of the disheveled Joanne and clinging child touched Ames deeply and he glanced at Kenton. The pain he saw behind the other man's wan smile told him much.

"Let me take the child," Lord Kenton said quietly, stepping forward. "She has done well and we must give her a biscuit with lots of butter and jam—and the rest of that hot chocolate."

Ellen turned her head, her face wreathed in a smile, and reached out.

Taking her, Kenton swung her up in the air and around to his back. The oil lamp was retrieved as soon as Ellen had secured her hold. "Dr. Ames—please take Lady Joanne's arm—we wouldn't want her to fall.

"Ladies," he nodded at the other two, "if you will follow me, let us return to warmth."

". . . so you see, it was not Ellen's fault. When the door blew shut, accidentally dropping the bar, there was no way she could reach it." Joanne smiled across at Ellen, ensconced on Kenton's lap and happily licking the last of the butter and jam from her fingers.

"She must have been too frightened to try to bring someone to me." Shuddering, she finished, "I know that feeling far too well to hold it against her."

Dr. Ames watched as Kenton's eyes snapped from the child nestling in his lap to Joanne as her voice altered with fear. They dropped when the young woman met his gaze.

"You must be famished, Lady Knoll," the matron said, finding an opening to speak at last. "It is long past the supper hour and . . ."

"Supper," exclaimed Joanne. "The party . . ."

"It will be held on the week next. Excuses have long since been sent," Lord Kenton said with a smile. "But, Mrs. Brasmen is correct. It is long past time for eating and Mrs. Caern will be worried into a pother if we delay longer.

"Dr. Ames, I would appreciate it if you would bring Lady Knoll to Kentoncombe."

"Of course, Lord Kenton. It is little enough," Ames answered.

"Let me help you put her to bed," Joanne said as Kenton rose with the now sleeping child in his arms. "I owe her much." Again she saw the odd look in his lordship's eyes.

"Mrs. Brasmen will show you to her bed," Dr. Ames put in when the silence held as the two stood gazing at each other. "I will have the carriage and mounts brought to the door."

"We will be a moment only," Kenton said. "Mrs. Brasmen, if you will."

With a wag of her knowing brows, the large woman padded forward. What goings on—in front of her very own eyes.

* * *

"I still do not understand why he had to be so sharp about it," Lady Joanne complained uneasily to Dr. Ames as he guided the horse carefully on the muddy track.

"It simply would not have been proper—besides he was thinking of your health," Ames returned.

"Bah, Jason—Lord Kenton, that is, knows I care not whether the weather be good or bad—or what others think for all that. The rain has ended; the night is clear. It would have been exhilarating to ride. Asteron would have taken my weight without complaint," she ended pettishly.

"And you would have taken a chill," laughed the young physician, suddenly happy his infatuation with this curiously unconventional young woman had not been returned. His chances from the beginning had been slight at best—who was he to hope for the daughter of an earl? The more he pondered the thought that had come to him upon seeing Lord Kenton and Lady Joanne's fervent embrace, the more instances occurred to verify his growing belief. "What did you say, my lady?" he asked, realizing she had spoken to him

"Where are your thoughts, Dr. Ames? And must I call you Dr. Ames? It is all so very formal. Why, I do not even know your given name."

"It is Benjamin, my lady, and I would be most pleased to have you use it—if you promise never to voice it in front of Mrs. Brasmen."

Laughter burst from both at the thought of the effect of such informality upon the somber matron.

"Can't you just see her—she would puff up and those brows of hers would wag worse than a pup's tail," Joanne managed, gasping for air. "It is too sad we shan't see it."

"No," said Ames, suddenly becoming serious. "Your reputation as well as my own would be harmed. Lord Kenton's friendship has done much for me—I would not see it so betrayed."

"By such a silly thing as my using your given name?" Joanne asked unbelievingly.

"It would not take so much as that—a look, an action can be misinterpreted."

"But I care for you . . . think of you as . . . as a brother," she said indignantly.

"You are most gracious," the young physician smiled and decided to change the direction of their conversation. "My lady."

"You needn't sound so priggish." The hurt sounded in Joanne's voice.

"Indeed, I did not mean to be," he answered, at once contrite. "It is an honour you do me in saying such."

"Then I may call you Benjamin?"

"When no one else is about—I suppose it would do."

"You are almost worse than Lord Jason," she scolded lightly, but happy to have his friendship confirmed. "Everyone must be proper—eat correctly, speak correctly, even curtsy correctly. Sometimes I could scream."

"And most likely do," he rejoined.

Joanne swatted his hand lightly. "That is unkind."

"True—not unkind. But forgive me, my lady. I venture too far, for I am *not* your brother."

"Oh, how I wish you were," she sighed, suddenly sad, "for then I could seek your advice."

Ames tried to read her features in the bobbing of the carriage light. "It would be a privilege if you would consider me such—or at least think of me as a true friend."

"Could I?"

Her eagerness struck him and he wondered as he had often done of her hunger for commendation or any sign of affection.

"There is much you do not know of me," Joanne went on when he did not speak. "Things that I could never speak of—they would shock you so."

"Then they must be from the past, which is best forgotten unless happy. You need never speak of it— tell me what troubles you now," he urged.

There was a long silence, broken only by the sucking slop of the hooves as the horse plodded through the mud and by the jingle of the harness.

At last Joanne began weakly. "It's Lord Jason . . . oh, I have been horrid to him. More than you can ever guess." Words tumbled over one another in their haste to be spoken. "He is and has been so kind and patient and with no reason to be such. More than anyone in my life, he has done for me . . . and I do not know how to tell him."

"Tell him? You wish to thank him?" Ames asked somewhat confused by her words.

"No . . . well, yes—but more than that. You see it was all rather nightmarish when I came to Kentoncombe and . . . and I thought I . . . hated him—told him I did. But this night when I could do naught but dwell on my life, I realized that I love him."

Beside her the young physician broke into a beaming smile.

". . . love him like a father, of course," Joanne continued. "What is wrong?" she asked as Ames choked and coughed. She pounded him upon the back.

"I am fine, fine now," he insisted. "You say you love Lord Kenton as a father?" he asked skeptically.

"Of course, as a father," Joanne answered brightly. "Why he is as old as my father. Well, perhaps not that old, but let us forget that. How do I tell him what I have discovered? At first I resolved to be absolutely good and very proper just as he would have me. I planned not to speak back—you saw how long that resolve held. I am afraid my tongue does seem to run afoul whenever Lord Jason and I disagree," she sighed.

"Even when you agree, from what I have heard," Ames added with a low chuckle.

"Now that is too much, even for a brother," laughed Joanne, then sobered. "But how am I to tell him, Benjamin?"

Desperately, Ames wished for time to think, time to decide what he should reveal of his thoughts, but Joanne was staring expectantly at him. He weighed his choices and chose delay. "In truth, I would not tell him anything. Lord Kenton would be . . ." he groped for words ". . . be embarrassed, shall we say. Let time wear awhile on this feeling you have discovered. Emotions oft are better aged, like wine, and let come to their fullness. There is much you can do to show the new regard you hold him in."

"What can I do?" Joanne broke in exasperatedly.

"Why, behave for one thing." Ames forced a laugh, breaking her seriousness.

"Perhaps you are correct," she answered. "I shall think on it. I do thank you for your thoughts. I have never had a friend, much less a brother, before."

Her sincerity caused him to reply, "I will always be happy and willing to be of assistance." He flicked the reins, prodding the horse from its slow plod.

A comradely silence engulfed the pair for the remainder of the journey. Soon Kentoncombe was before them—a blaze of light in the darkness. Seeing that men awaited the arrival of the carriage, Joanne laid her hand upon Ames's arm. "You will not speak of what I have told you?" she asked.

"Not if you do not wish me to."

"Oh, thank you. I would be quite out of charity with you if you did."

"And we mustn't have that," he teased lightly as he drew the horse to a halt before Kentoncombe's door.

"Oh, mustn't we," returned Joanne archly and both shared the laughter of a common jest not noticing Lord Kenton had emerged and stood watching.

He took in their happy faces and shared laughter, saw Joanne's hand resting on Ames's arm. A deep sorrow settled upon his heart, blotting out the faint hope it held.

Chapter Fourteen

The crisp cool air of fall turned into the chillier winds of winter. Joanne chose to follow Dr. Ames's advice and spoke not to Kenton, but none could fail to notice the increased effort she put into her lessons.

Lord Kenton changed imperceptibly, growing more formal. He avoided being alone with Joanne for long periods and found every excuse to throw Joanne and Dr. Ames together. He maintained his friendship while avoiding any conversation on the subject of Joanne.

Only observations of his lordship at unguarded moments continued to convince Ames that Kenton was keeping his true feelings for her under tight rein.

Mrs. Caern watched the trio with growing unease. Only Lady Joanne was untouched, not comprehending the undercurrents about her, certain she had found a substitute father.

Meticulously following the exercise and dietary course set by Kenton, Joanne slimmed even more. Shortly after Christmas the dressmaker was summoned to Kentoncombe once more.

This dear lady was sadly confused as she came from Joanne's bedchamber. Mrs. Caern had directed her to measure and discuss styles for the young lady's day gowns, pelisses, evening gowns, and many smaller items—so many in fact that the seamstress had been somewhat concerned at the size of the task. Lady Knoll, however, had just told her to make only three day gowns, one warm and durable—imagine a young lady wanting something durable—and one gown for evening wear. Worse still, Lady Joanne had selected common materials, not at all the sort the gentry chose for putting on their airs. Uncertain of what to do, Mrs. Daniels paused worriedly outside the coat-of-arms chamber door.

Lord Kenton, coming from his study, approached her, and the sturdy little seamstress bobbed a hasty curtsy.

Seeing she was upset, he halted. "Mrs. Daniels, is it not? Can I be of help?"

"It concerns her ladyship's instructions, milord. Mrs. Caern told me there would be a large number of gowns and other articles to be made and that they were to be of the more expensive materials. But Lady Knoll ordered only four gowns and these of my least costly cloth."

Brow furrowed in puzzlement, Kenton pondered the seamstress's words. "You have all the measurements needed for any gown?" he asked.

"Oh, yes, milord."

"Then I suggest you begin on one of the gowns her ladyship ordered and delay starting on the remainder until a message is sent to you. A minor misunderstanding seems to have come about."

"Thank you, milord." Mrs. Daniels gave him a relieved smile. "I best be going." Bobbing another quick curtsy, she stepped briskly on her way.

Remaining before Joanne's chamber door, Kenton deliberated on the cause behind Joanne's orders to the seamstress. *She has decided to wed Ames* came first to his mind. No, he reasoned, that made no sense, for she believes the garments are paid for by her father. What can be the reason for so miserly a choice?

The door was too near, the question too demanding. Before Kenton could stay his hand, he found he was knocking upon the door.

The rein he had kept upon his heart was sorely tried by the image his eyes met upon its opening. A deep lavender morning gown, simply cut and unadorned, was wrapped around Joanne's figure, revealing the natural body lines. His eyes followed the soft curves with a hunger long suppressed. Her brown hair hung in soft velvet waves upon her shoulders. A maidenly blush heightened her looks as her brown eyes widened in surprise.

"Lord Jason, I had no idea . . . I thought it must be Mrs. Daniels. We just finished . . ." she said, seeking to explain why she was not dressed at such a late morning hour.

"I know," he acknowledged, his mind far from his words. "I just spoke with her myself. In fact it is what she told me that makes me admit to some puzzlement. I . . ." Words died as his eyes feasted, his heart raced. All his reasoning and suppressing had done naught. Love pulsed so strongly, he felt she must see it, feel it. How was it to be denied? Unknowingly he stepped closer. Standing before him, guileless, she drew him with a passion he had hoped to deny. Mentally Kenton cursed. Circumstances bound him, moral precepts held him fast in speech and act to the sham of a tutor.

Taking in his gaze, Joanne felt once again the strange sensation of excitement that came whenever he was near. *Odd that he should appear before my door just when I am trying to puzzle through my growing need to be close to him,* she thought as her pulse quickened. A longing to reach out and touch his face filled her. The desire to be held once more in his arms began to consume her.

Neither was aware of Kenton's incompleted thought as they stood wrapped in tormenting emotions. His lordship's discipline broke and for a moment passion flickered in his steady brown eyes.

An answering spirit leaped within Joanne. She leaned toward him and was seared by the anger that flashed into his eyes. *Why? What have I done wrong?* she thought despairingly.

Joanne's look of total vulnerability tested Kenton too far. If he stayed a moment more he would take her in his arms. "Come to my study when you have dressed," he blurted like a schoolboy, turning on heel and fleeing with as much dignity as his hammering heart would allow.

Reaching his study, he paced about, mentally reciting the litany of his foolishness. The tolerability of the situation had been broken at last. From the night he had rescued Joanne and held her in his arms he had been forced to admit his love. The caress of his name on her lips, the love in her eyes, and the intimacy of her manner made him loosen his stranglehold on a hope he held futile. Did she love him? With crushing clarity the question was answered by Joanne's naive eagerness to please. It came, not surprisingly but quellingly to his heart, that she viewed him as a father, that her trust was centered in thinking of him as such. In becoming her tutor he had contrived a gaol for his own love.

He shook himself, glancing at the letter lying open upon the desk before him, his lips tightening into a frown. No ordinary missive that, he thought, but the tool of reality. A surge of anger made him crumple the letter in his hand. Delivered but a week past, it had torn Kenton from his half world of "mayhaps" into the world of facts. It was now time to halt the self-pity, he told himself, and to think of Joanne's welfare.

He had debated ignoring the date set by Furness for Joanne's journey to London, but the power of the law was behind the earl. He could demand and procure Joanne's return. A confrontation with her father would crush Joanne's new self-confidence, Kenton was certain, and simply sending her to the man would never do. Neither would having her remain at Kentoncombe do, he realized, after this morn. To have her stay would ultimately test him too far. A time would come when he would not be able to restrain himself. He could not bear it if Joanne came to distrust him—to hate him because of it. In no way was she responsible for the trap he now found himself in. She was innocent of enticement, of flirting. The few sallies he had weakly ventured had all met with questioning puzzlement on her part.

During the past two months Kenton had come to know much of Joanne's childhood. He marveled at how matter-of-factly she spoke, often not realizing what she was revealing. Knowledge of Lord Furness's treatment of his daughter ended hopes Kenton had harboured that he might yet speak to her of his love. Vilely misused by her natural father, it was unalterably confirmed in Kenton's mind that Joanne could only be harmed further if the daughterly trust she had placed in him was betrayed. *Lord, you're almost of an age to be her father,* he sarcastically reminded himself. Besides, there are far better prospects than you can offer awaiting her in London.

A light tapping aroused Kenton. It must be Joanne. He would do as his conscience bid him. "Enter," he called out.

Joanne stepped into the room slowly and sat in the chair beside his desk. The onslaught of emotion had left her shaken, confused. Questions had tumbled through her mind. The realization that she loved Jason, not as a father, but as a man, smote her. Suddenly the peculiarity of her recent emotions became clear. A second realization hit with sickening force. *He has thrown Benjamin and me together constantly these two months past,* she thought, *and turned so cold and proper. Does he wish to be rid of me— even to the extent of forcing a match with Benjamin?* She awaited Kenton's words tremulously.

"I must ask you a question," he began slowly. "It is personal," he dropped his eyes for a moment, then raised them to hers, "but, as I have assumed responsibility for your welfare, I must have an answer. Do you have a *tendre* for Ames?" He ended in a rush, glad to have it out.

"I care for Benjamin as I would a brother, had I

one," Joanne answered, her eyes not wavering from Kenton's. She would not be forced into a match.

"You have no desire to wed him?" he persisted.

"No," she clipped out. He did hope to be rid of her as she had thought.

"I see," his fingers drummed upon the desk. Then he reached out and drew forward a large leather-bound book from one side and opened it to a marked page. As he looked at the page before him, Kenton asked, "Do you know of family other than your aunt, Lady Evelyn?"

"No, but why do you ask?"

"I have received a letter from your father." Kenton winced as he saw her blanch. "He seeks news of your progress."

"Why?" she asked coldly.

"The time set for your leaving Kentoncombe draws near."

"Leaving?" Joanne raised her hand to still the sudden pounding of her heart. "Surely you do not wish me to depart? Has the money he left been spent? If so I can do without the new gowns and . . . and there must be some way, something I can do to earn my way here," she pleaded.

Kenton steeled his heart. "It is not a question of money. It was set before your arrival that you would stay only till March. You were to learn what you would need to know for a London season in that time."

"You would hand me over to my father knowing what he is? What he has done to me in the past? Is there nothing I can say or do to alter your decision?"

"The decision was never mine to make. You are a

young woman—the daughter of an earl. In London you shall experience the things all young women desire. You shall find a husband and make a home."

"I want neither husband nor home," Joanne cried, rising, tears brimming. "I am happy here. Why can I not stay? I will do whatever you ask. I know I can do better than I have. Please do not make me return to him." Joanne broke into sobs.

Bending his resolve, Kenton rose and wrapped his arms reassuringly about her—he could not bear the pain he saw upon her. "You *must* go to London come March," he repeated as much to himself as to her, "but I will see that it is not to your father you go." He raised her chin in his hand, forcing her to look at him. "Dry those tears—Mrs. Caern will wonder what is about," he tried to tease, hoping she could not hear his pounding heart. As she reached for his kerchief, he stepped back. "Now, that is better. I want you to send a message to Mrs. Daniels asking her to make only two of the day gowns you ordered, but of a finer cloth. Have one pelisse made and be certain it is lined with fur. And tell her she shall be paid for the entire order—even those things not now required."

Yes, he said to himself, *it will be better to wait and see what . . .* he shook his head and let the thought die uncompleted. "There is a journey I must make," Kenton began anew. "Continue your lessons and your work at Irwin." He smiled reassuringly at Joanne's fearful, questioning look. "I shall not be gone long. But we must discuss this further when I return."

"When shall you be leaving?"

"In the morn."

"Not so soon?"

"You are not to worry—I will see that Ames keeps check on you. You must excuse me now, for I must be about the trip's preparations."

Joanne nodded and watched him go. Plopping dejectedly into his chair, she turned and faced the windows. Was it all to end—the peace, the happiness?

How can I face my father? London? she asked herself, fear welling within once more. How can Jason arrange for me to go to any other? Surely he could not mean for me to go to Aunt Evelyn? She looked down at the large volume open before her. A glance showed it to be Burke's listing of the aristocratic and landed families of England. Further investigation revealed it was open to the pages citing the Furness title.

Why had he looked to this—what did it mean?

Chapter Fifteen

"The coach, Benjamin, the coach!" Joanne said excitedly as the pair topped the hill before Kentoncombe. "He has returned. Hurry!"

Ames urged the horse to a faster pace in answer to the eager joy he saw upon her features.

Bounding out of the gig before Ames could halt it entirely, Joanne raced to the coach.

"They be inside, milady," Ben told her as he directed the removal of the last of the baggage.

They, she thought, entering the foyer. Who could have come with Jason?

"His lordship has returned, milady." Nell greeted Joanne in the foyer, reaching out to take her heavy cloak. "He said you were to come to the library as soon as you have freshened up."

"Who is with him?"

"To the truth, milady, no one knows. All bundled up she was and right to the library they went—secret like," the young maid gossiped.

Relief filled Joanne—it was not her father. But who, then? Curiosity turned her steps not to her chamber but toward the library. Patting stray wisps of hair in place, she half ran to it. Enough vanity had been instilled that she paused for a moment outside the doors and tugged her skirt straight before bursting into the room.

At sight of the diminutive figure seated beside Lord Kenton she froze.

"You said she was somewhat impulsive," a lyrical voice noted. "You are proven correct. I can see my task will be somewhat strenuous."

"Then you agree to my plan?" Kenton asked, drinking in Joanne's beauty.

"How could I refuse, seeing her. It will be a most interesting season. Who knows, she may even attract someone I may be able to snare." The voice broke into tinkling laughter.

Shock was turning to anger when Kenton rose and took Joanne's hand. The warmth of his touch banished the anger, the woman momentarily forgotten as her heart thrilled to have him near once more. "I am so glad you are home," she said returning the pressure of his grip.

"And I," he returned. Giving himself a mental shake, for he longed to put his arms about Joanne, he continued, "But I must introduce you to our guest."

The glimmer of triumph in Lord Jason's voice unconsciously irked Joanne more than the woman's resemblance to her mother had shaken her.

"Here is someone who has been most anxious to meet you," Kenton told Joanne. "I present you to your aunt, Pauline, Comtesse de Clarté."

The comtesse rose and stepped forward to embrace

Joanne, who backed away. Only Kenton's grip upon her hand kept her in the library.

"My child, what is wrong?" the comtesse asked, her hurt plainly visible. "You cannot know my joy at learning Joanna had a daughter. I was in France when she married Furness—a tragic mistake on her part.

"I have been in London these five years past—ever since my husband, the dear comte, passed away." She sighed sadly. "But enough of me. Imagine my surprise when Lord Kenton appeared at my door and told me of your existence!" she said, her hands fluttering gracefully.

Joanne's eyes went from the small delicate figure to Lord Kenton. The stern frown there sent them back to the first. "I . . . I am . . . pleased to meet you," she stammered and her hand was freed.

A cough from the corridor turned all to face Dr. Ames. "I wished to add my welcome upon your return, my lord," he said to Kenton while taking in the unknown lady appreciatively.

"Thank you, Benjamin. May I introduce Lady Joanne's aunt, the Comtesse de Clarté. Comtesse, this is Dr. Ames. He has established a foundling home at Irwin Manor and visits us oft."

"Most charmed, Comtesse," Ames said, bowing deeply. "Your coming will brighten the dull moments of this winter for all of us."

Eyes twinkling, the comtesse gave a coquettish wink. "Most flattering, *Docteur*. I look forward to becoming better acquainted with you."

"An excellent prospect, but alas, now I must excuse

myself. There are several calls I must make before this eve." He bowed once more to the comtesse, turned, and shook hands with Kenton. "Glad to have you back—Lady Joanne has been most anxious for your safe return," Ames said to him, trying to give a hint of how things really lay. "Word has come that General Howe drove the colonial army from Trenton in early December." He cocked his head and with a wry grin continued, "But Dr. Fowler was not pleased, for the same letter told how General Washington had retaken the city in less than three weeks. Now he is for Parliament raising our taxes and impressing more unfortunates to be sent to reinforce Howe. Enough, let us keep this for later discussion. I am already late. Lady Joanne," he nodded.

"I will walk with you to the door, Benjamin," Joanne said, looking challengingly at Kenton as she spoke the physician's given name.

The younger couple gone, the comtesse looked gravely at Lord Kenton. "The child will not accept me."

"Joanne is not a child," Kenton spoke more sharply than he meant to. "Willful like a child at times, and certainly guileless in the ways of society—of men, but no child."

The comtesse raised her brows, a faint smile playing upon her lips. "No," she said slowly, "she is not a child. But that does not alter the matter. Perhaps it only increases the difficulty."

"Please do not give up before you have even begun. I believe it is your resemblance to her mother that has upset her. Furness has tossed her mother's beauty and grace at Joanne since birth and she has not always possessed the looks that she now has. If you could have seen her when she came to Kentoncombe you would realize what progress she has made. I cannot overstress how misused she has been. There will be only tragedy for her if she must return to her father. He will destroy all the changes that have been wrought. In your care and with your guidance she will have a successful season. You must do this."

Once again she wondered at the cause of this man's intensity when speaking of Joanne or the glow in his eye when she had appeared. Only parents were this caring—or lovers. . . . "I have not said I would not, my lord. Ease your mind. The challenge shall prove most exhilarating—a respite from my dull widow's life," the comtesse sighed.

Several days passed and once again the comtesse and Lord Kenton spoke of Joanne.

"But you must see how much she dislikes the idea." The delicate face frowned. His lordship was being very thickheaded. "Why must she go to London? Would not the young *docteur* take her to wife?" she asked lightly.

Kenton's eyes narrowed. "She insists she cares for him only as a brother."

"But what of yourself?"

"Myself?" Kenton repeated, masking his features, despite his shock at the question.

"Why, yes. It is not uncommon for a man of your age to take a young wife and mold her as he desires. If the two of you deal well together, and from what I have seen you do, why not marry?" she ended matter-of-factly.

"Because she thinks of me as a father," Kenton answered with dry honesty. How could he explain he was being torn by his decision not to press his unwelcome suit on Joanne. That he believed his doing so would harm her, or worse, bring her to hate him.

"Oh . . . oh!" the comtesse said pensively. "But I am certain that is not . . . never mind my chatter." It was very evident that Lord Kenton believed what he had said. *Men are such fools,* she thought.

Rising, she walked to where he stood in the center of the room. Taking both his hands in her small delicate fingers she said, "All will be right for her—I will do my best to see to that."

"Thank you, my lady." The emotion rang deep in his voice as he bowed and raised one of her hands to his lips. The rustle of skirts behind him as he did so announced Joanne's presence.

"Lady Joanne, we were just speaking of you. The comtesse wishes to move her things to the Queen Anne bedchamber—she will be much closer to you there," Kenton told her.

And to you, thought Joanne, recalling the image of Kenton kissing the comtesse's hand.

The older woman noted this but hid her mild amusement. *Rarely have I seen the actions of a "father" arouse jealousy,* she thought. This shall prove most *intéressant.*

The frigid air blown in from the coast began to thaw as February ended. The first day of March saw the first bright sunshine bathe the land.

Wrapping her warm pelisse about her, Joanne

sought the refuge of the gardens. Still decked in winter browns and yellows, the area showed the promise of spring only in a few wild snowbells, which stood bravely in scattered clumps. Finding a sun-warmed bench, she sat and stared at the crisp white bell-shaped flowers, contemplating a future she saw as bleak.

Only two weeks, she thought, *two weeks and I am to go.* Her eyes swept over the familiar grounds; every shrub, stepping stone, and planting design had been memorized in her many hours of walking about. *How can I go? I love him.*

Tears crowded to the brim of Joanne's eyes. Night after night she had searched desperately for some way to forestall the journey to London. The comtesse was insistent that they must go early so that both could be gowned, coiffed, and jeweled for the approaching season. Joanne fingered the golden rose about her neck—Kenton's Michaelmas gift. *Why couldn't it have been a gift of his love,* she thought, *Why can I not remain here?* A lone tear trailed down her cheek.

A small gloved hand touched the tear lightly and it was gone. Joanne started in surprise.

"May I sit with you?" the comtesse asked.

In answer Joanne moved to one side of the bench.

"The tear—you are sad, *n'est-ce pas?* Could you not tell me why?"

Shaking her head, Joanne touched the corner of each eye, drying the tears trembling there.

"But perhaps I could help. Please? Your sadness troubles me deeply."

For once Joanne did not shrug off her aunt's words.

Turning, she looked at the comtesse squarely, searchingly, not belligerently nor angrily as she had so oft since the other's coming, but questioningly.

"Give me but the chance and you shall see my friendship is true," the older woman entreated. "Is it that you do not believe I knew not of your existence until Lord Kenton told me?"

Joanne shook her head. She believed the comtesse—even liked much about her vivacious, openhearted aunt, but . . . But what? she questioned herself now, forced by the distress she saw in the other. "I believe you," she said, "but . . . oh, I don't know. In truth, I do like you."

A delighted "oh" broke from the other. "If you can like me—then you may come to love me." The comtesse reached out and took Joanne's hand. "Now tell me the cause of the tears."

"You know I cannot bear to leave Kentoncombe," broke from Joanne.

"But why?" came back the familiar challenge which had oft caused Joanne to wonder during the past six weeks if she knew any other. "Do I not understand it correctly that you have been here only—what? Five, no, eight months?"

Eight months, thought Joanne. *Rather a lifetime.* She nodded.

"What is there here to recommend itself so dear to your heart? The weather—certainly not! The features of the land? The people? No. None of these can bind you to this place after so brief a stay. I myself lived in France seven and ten years and left it with only a slight regret. All that held me to France was my dear comte."

Her eyes softened in remembrance. "Is there such a one to hold you here?" she asked softly.

A quick shake of her head gave answer as Joanne rose. She dared not speak of her love for Jason. "You do not understand."

"How am I to understand without your aid?" the comtesse returned sharply. "I came here for one reason—to help you. And what have you given me in return?" After letting the question settle, she continued sadly. "Oh, but I am the fool. The useless one. With no children of my own to teach me, I know not what to do. Everything I venture you misunderstand."

"No, Aunt," came from Joanne. "It is I, not you. From my birth I have been told how useless I am." An almost forgotten bitterness returned in her words.

The comtesse leaped to her feet and grabbed Joanne by the arms—the younger woman being over a head taller. "You must not say that—not ever again," she exclaimed. "I forbid it! You are a lovely woman—young, with much to offer. Your father destroyed my sister, your mother—do not let him do the same to you." Tears spilled freely.

Joanne at last realized the caring behind the words, the love that flowed with the tears. She released her own pent-up tears and hugged her aunt desperately.

When the deluge was spent, they separated and dabbed at their eyes. Glancing at one another, they burst into laughter and, linking arms, began a slow walk back to the manor house.

"No more tears for us, Joanne," the comtesse ordered brightly. "We are going to London—yes," she said. "There is no other way and one must bow to fate gracefully—but, do not fear. I know you shall see Kentoncombe once again. So, we shall journey to London and enjoy ourselves famously, *n'est-ce pas?*"

A weak nod came from Joanne.

"That will not do. You must believe it—make the best of it. Think of the balls, ridottos, soirées we shall attend. The young men shall flock to see the daughter of the hellion Furness and what a surprise we shall give them. They will gather about you and that cannot be but pleasure for me also." She winked coquettishly, drawing a smile from Joanne. "That is much better. And do not worry on account of your father—he is no match for the pair of us. No one will be," she laughed thinking of Kenton. "Let us go now and look through the pages of *The Ladies Magazine*. We must decide on our gowns and of course whether we will use feathers or ribbons, pearls or even grapes in our periwigs.

"Laugh if you will," she challenged and then laughed also. "Pooh, but there are many foolish things you shall see. Why once . . ."

Joanne let the words wash over her. Perhaps the comtesse was correct and she would enjoy "society." Better to contemplate furbelows and geegaws than . . .

"You are not listening, Joanne." The comtesse tweaked her on the arm. "Do you think puce or river blue more becoming to my colouring? Of course for you we shall choose vibrant hues." The comtesse paused and put a finger to her lips, suddenly deep in thought. *"Oui,"* she continued smiling broadly, "you shall enjoy your season immensely—just as I did ever

so long ago. For me there was the comte. For you—
ah, for you believe me or no, there is someone equally
special and just as conquerable in the time known as
'the Season.' "

Chapter Sixteen

The harsh-faced figure rose disgustedly, slapping his losing cards down roughly upon the table. Wordlessly he strode to the doors where the attendant handed him his hat and gloves.

"May I walk with you?" Wiltham called, wending his way between the gaming tables.

Furness walked out, not answering.

Unabashed, Wiltham followed, catching up with the earl as he proceeded down the street. "Your game has not been good of late," he noted. "Perhaps it is not so much that luck has deserted you as that your concentration is not what it should be. You appear to be distracted of late—can I be of assistance?"

A dark look from his companion silenced Wiltham.

Halting suddenly, Furness signaled a sedan chair. Before he stepped in, he ordered curtly, "Follow me to my apartments."

Wiltham watched the bobbing movement of the link boy's torch ahead of Furness's sedan for a moment. Breaking into a jubilant smile, he signaled one for himself and directed them to take him to Furness's London dwelling.

Patience, my man, patience, Wiltham told himself, swirling the drink in his glass while he observed Furness draw yet another.

"I have heard you are in need of funds," Furness broke the silence. "There may be a way for you to have all you require—for the past and the future."

"Yes, my lord?" Wiltham questioned, hoping his excitement did not show. At last it appeared he was near his long-sought goal.

Pouring another drink, Furness continued, "I have a daughter."

"Strange that I had not heard anyone speak of her," Wiltham noted. "Children can be such a blessing." He stared at his glass.

"Blessing," spat Furness. "More a curse." He waved his hand angrily and downed another drink. "I wish to be rid of her—to be free from thinking of her ever again."

"Is the child deformed then?"

"No. No longer a child either."

"And I may be of help?" Wiltham asked innocently.

"An arrangement could be reached that would solve both our problems," Furness said, filling the other's glass. "Are you interested?" he asked by way of mere formality. His agents had had little trouble in learning the extent of Wiltham's financial peril.

"My lord," the younger man frowned, "you know I would do anything to help you. Have I not shown that in the year just past?"

A sudden tingling doubt brought a frown to the older man. Was it wise to endure Wiltham just for this one end? Was there not the possibility that Kenton and his wife would take pity on Joanne and wish her to remain with them? No. He would not risk it. He had to be certain she would never return to his own care. Oh, Joanna, had you but lived and this daughter died. A gleam of guilt at his present plans wormed its way into his thoughts.

"Just tell me what you wish," Wiltham prompted smoothly, disliking Furness's hesitation.

Gulping further port to fortify the "rightness" of his actions, Furness said, "On my part I will pay all your debts . . . and settle an allowance upon you."

"Most generous, my lord, but what shall you require of me?" Wiltham asked, now certain of the answer.

"In two—three weeks I shall be forced to bring my daughter to London—a lesson against rashness, I assure you. But I do not wish to be embarrassed by her presence," he continued. "You shall wed her upon her arrival and take her to your country estate, Wornstone. What you do with her I care not—so long as I never see nor hear of her again."

"Why should I wed one which arouses such harsh feelings? She cannot be pleasant," Wiltham noted, caution appearing for a second.

"Because you owe money to far too many. Refuse and I shall send the duns upon you. There should be no doubt what the result would be." Furness smiled wickedly.

For the first time fear entered Wiltham's mind. The plan he had followed so eagerly to free himself of debt was near culmination, but something was warning him to pull back. "What if she is not willing?" he asked, wavering at the last moment.

"She will not be given a choice." Finality rang in the words. "Do you agree?"

"There is much to consider . . ."

"Your answer," Furness commanded coldly.

Wiltham swallowed his doubts and nodded.

"Wise choice," Furness clipped. "I shall send my man around in the morn. Give him a listing of what and who you owe. There also will be a sum deposited in your name for current expenses at an establishment you select. Arrangements for the allowance shall be set the day you wed my daughter."

"May I ask the amount?" Wiltham ventured greedily.

"Let us say it shall be sufficient for you to settle your bride safely at Wornstone and then enjoy a grand honeymoon tour with someone . . . of your choice." Furness filled his glass again. *At last it would be over,* he thought. When she was wed, the demon he battled daily would be defeated. He rubbed his eyes heavily. Now it would not matter what sort of "education" Kenton had been able to instill in Joanne. Furness sat tiredly, leaning his head back against the plush-cushioned chair. "Leave me. All will be taken care of."

Thinking it wise not to press, Wiltham bowed and withdrew. His future at least was assured, or so he believed.

The adventure was about to begin but what a sad-faced lot was assembling to see it off. Mrs. Caern wiped a tear away as she saw to the loading of the baggage. She had come to love the troubled young miss, as had all the household servants. Lord Kenton had been scowling for a week and Lady Joanne had moped silently through the rooms and corridors.

The day had come at last and Lord Kenton and the comtesse were together for a last conference.

"Lord Kenton, you are too worrisome—something I find difficult to believe of you. I assure you, Lord Furness will not prove difficult. There is little he can do. It will not seem odd that I introduce his daughter into society, as he is a widower and I childless. He will probably be relieved to have the duty taken from his hands if all you say is true. Besides, we are agreed that no one shall know who Joanne is until the ball. Are you certain you shall not come?"

Kenton shook his head. "Remember—Furness is a vicious man and there is no telling what he will do."

"But the man still maintains the fringes of respect. When I introduce Joanne, he will have no choice but to leave her with me or cause a scandal. Do not be so gloomy," she smiled. "One would think you are losing more than a pair of houseguests. Is not the purpose of this venture to obtain a match for Joanne—to see her happily settled?"

"Only if it pleases her. I do not want her forced in any way."

"She shall be constrained in no way, my lord," the comtesse said mischievously. "I am certain there is some fine young buck who will win Joanne's heart."

To Kenton's ear, the lighthearted chatter held the barb of sarcasm. He studied her steadily. "You envision no problems then?"

"But why should there be any?" she twittered, rising. "The appointed departure hour draws near. There are a few details I must attend."

"Would you tell Lady Joanne I wish to speak with her here, privately, now?" he asked.

"Of course, my lord. She shall come in but a moment."

The laughing eyes seemed to be taunting, but he could not imagine why. Joanne's image had been blotting all else from his mind.

"My lord," a voice said softly as a hand touched Kenton's shoulder lightly. He stiffened, steeling himself for this scene. "I did not mean to startle you, my lord," Joanne said, "but your mind was very far from here. You did not hear me knock or enter."

Kenton drank in the vision she presented—the downy blue traveling suit making her a patch of spring sky so welcome after a long winter. The urge to take her in his arms was almost unbearable.

"You wished to see me?" she asked when he did not speak.

"Yes, Joanne . . . Lady Joanne," he corrected himself gruffly. "Be seated." Kenton motioned to the usual chair beside the desk.

How oft have I sat here and spoke to him, Joanne thought. *Why did it take so long to realize I loved him?* She blinked back the tears that came and raised her chin bravely. He did not care or he would never have let her go—she would not betray her feelings.

While Joanne seated herself, Kenton opened the center drawer and removed a dark, wine-stained leather pouch and two small carved wooden chests. "When your father stopped at Kentoncombe before your arrival, he gave me this," he said holding forth the pouch. "Of course some has been used—for your gowns and the pin money you have been given. What remains is rightfully yours to use as you see fit. Take it," Kenton ordered as she sat unmoving. "Keep it safe for the time when you need it."

"Thank you, my lord," Joanne answered, reaching out and taking the pouch gingerly. It was very heavy.

Kenton smiled at her surprise. "It is gold—watch it closely." His eyes dropped to the two chests upon the desk and his smile waned. Coughing, he cleared his throat, wishing the words would come. "I feel . . . I mean . . . Well, you are hardly a stranger here, Lady Joanne. All here at Kentoncombe hold you in fond thought." His eyes finally rose from the desk to meet hers. The unhappiness he saw there was echoed in his own. *I could make myself believe there is love in her eyes for me,* he thought. Hammering down his desire with an iron will, he continued.

"Therefore I have decided," he coughed, "decided a gift would be proper—in the name of all here at Kentoncombe, of course." The words out, he thrust the two chests at her.

If she had not been so close to tears, so upset and confused, Joanne would have found this sudden awkwardness at odds with Kenton's usual demeanour, would have recognized the strain he was under.

Taking the two, her hand touched his and the tremour of excitement that ran through her caused her to pull away quickly, unknowingly deepening the hurt in Kenton. "Shall I open them?" she asked in quavering tones, not daring to meet his eyes.

"If you like," Kenton replied with a strained voice.

Unsteadily, Joanne opened the larger of the two. A soft "ohh" came from her as she picked up the bracelet—the golden, hand-wrought roses attached upon two fine gold chains.

"You seemed pleased with the necklace and I thought this would complete the set," Kenton noted, smiling at her pleased expression. "You will have need of it now."

"It is beautiful, Jason," she breathed using only his given name as she did in her thoughts.

"Open the other," he prompted, his sorrow forgotten in her happiness.

The bracelet was laid reverently in place and the smaller chest slowly opened. The same gold rose sparkled at her—this time mounted on a ring. Trembling, she removed it and held it out. "Would you ... would you place it upon my hand?"

Neither noticed it was her left hand she held out. Swallowing a gulp, Kenton took the ring and eased it on. He held the hand longer than necessary, staring at the ring—he who longed to put a much plainer gold band upon that same finger.

"Come, come," called the comtesse, throwing the study door open. She paused at the sight of the two—hand in hand. "We must be off," she twittered gaily, forcing the two to notice her. "Why, what is that you have, Joanne?" she asked to ease the moment.

Kenton released the hand and Joanne threw a pain-stricken look at her aunt. The comtesse hardened her heart. This pair would have to suffer for a bit longer. "Such beautiful gifts—they match the necklace, do they not? But we must not tarry. Put them in your reticule. Here, I have brought it and your pelisse."

Taking the wrap from the comtesse, Kenton gently placed it upon Joanne's shoulders.

The older woman took the younger's hand and led the way. When they reached the carriage, she maneuvered it so Kenton handed Joanne in first. As he assisted her, she smiled brightly. "I do hope you change your mind about coming. It would please me very much. Promise me you shall think on it?"

He nodded. "And you promise to inform me if Furness should cause any problem," he said slowly.

At that moment Dr. Ames's gig clattered down the road. He jumped from it as a groom snatched the horse's bridle. "I feared I would miss you," he gasped, quite out of breath from his trip and the dash to the coach's side. "Mrs. Sidney has a son—I feared for a time the birth would make me too late but the babe arrived and I am happily come. My lady," he said bowing and kissing the comtesse's hand.

"I shall miss you, Dr. Ames—perhaps you can persuade Lord Kenton to come to London and join him on his journey."

"I shall try," he assured her.

"Till we meet again then," she smiled and impulsively kissed his cheek. "*Adieu.*"

Kenton took the comtesse's hand to help her into the coach and Ames turned to Joanne, who sat leaning her head out the open window. She reached out and he took her hand, kissing it. "Take care, Sister."

"And you." She squeezed his hand. "Look after him for me?"

He nodded.

Slamming the coach door, Kenton signaled Ben to start out. All from the manor house had gathered around and waved as the coach swayed up the hill, then was gone.

"They are on their way," Ames noted.

"Yes," Kenton said tiredly. Then, "Come—join me in a glass of port."

"Not so early in the day," laughed Ames. "No, I am for home and bed. But I shall sup with you this eve."

"I may not be able to sup," Kenton clipped sternly, "but come if you will."

Ames pressed Kenton's shoulder, giving him a hard look before he left. His friend was taking it hard. He hoped the comtesse was right—that all would be well in the end.

Chapter Seventeen

Tight-lipped, cheeks furrowed into a deep frown, Lady Joanne Knoll endured still another pinprick.

"Sorry, milady," the seamstress mumbled through the mouthful of pins. " 'Tis almost done."

"Thank God," Joanne returned.

The woman kneeling at the hem shook her head. Usually the young ones weren't so bold with their tongues as this one. But then she was older than most just come to London. Having learned to hold her tongue long ago, the seamstress turned her thoughts back to her work. Needle and thread darted in and out of the green water-silk gown like an adder through the grass. The last stitch in place, she sighed and rose. "That'll be all for now, my lady." Wrinkled, pinpricked hands unfastened the buttons, then dropped to the seamstress's side as Joanne motioned her away. It was a most curious fact that this particular young lady shrugged off—no, repelled—assistance, disrobing and dressing herself.

"Will they be ready on the day set?" questioned Joanne.

"Of course, milady," the seamstress said with a curtsy. Long nights and short candles to be sure until Thursday, was her thought.

"Bring them as soon as you complete the last. I shall take the petticoats and other undergarments with me now."

"Yes, milady. I will ready them for you. Only a moment please," the seamstress excused herself.

"The fittings are done I see." The comtesse greeted her niece, coming into the room like a bright ray of light.

Joanne made a face and nodded. "Well it is the last," she snapped. "I have seen enough of cloth, seamstress, milliner, feathers—all of it!"

"But why?" laughed the comtesse teasingly. "These things make life worthwhile. Recall, your goal is to snare a lord who is rich enough to ensure a lifetime of shopping. What would life be if we could not spend our time thusly?"

"More enjoyable," Joanne stated adamantly.

"We are almost at an end of it for a time, at least," her aunt comforted her. "Do you not enjoy it—even a little?" she asked, her curiosity winning out.

"Mayhap—at least at the beginning, but it has grown so tiresome. I feel like a cat who rolled into a bunch of nettles and for what—to be groomed like a filly for sale. Constantly pinched and poked about—I would almost wear what I have. The little seamstress from Ilfracombe was not so clumsy. Oh, for the peace of my days at . . ."

"Truly, Joanne, you must stop this . . . this sniffling about over Kentoncombe. There is many a girl who longs to be in your circumstance—to be in London about to be launched into society at a grand ball."

"But I do not want to be," interrupted Joanne. "It all seems more to the style of showing a brood mare from what you have told me. I have no intention of being chosen like some . . . oh." Words halted and her lip quivered. Tears were blinked back.

"You shall feel better after a few days' rest. This is all new to you. It would be most enjoyable if you gave yourself half a chance. Do you not wish Lord Kenton to be proud of you?"

The quivering lip hardened in angry lines. "He is not even thinking of me—why should I of him?" she snapped. Grabbing the boxes of garments from the startled seamstress's helper, she stalked from the chamber.

The comtesse followed hurriedly. "You must not do this. Always have your things carried for you and slow your steps," she commanded. "The pace is much too unladylike."

Already Joanne was sorry for her outburst. "I am sorry, Aunt. You have gone to so much trouble for me and I continue to be horridly ungrateful. I do try you terribly, I know."

"Let us say your approach to matters is a bit different from mine. It has kept my life interesting these past weeks." Since she was still a step behind Joanne, the comtesse indulged in a highly pointed expression —interesting indeed.

"We are finished with the shopping, are we not?" Joanne asked hopefully.

"Yes, my dear, we are. We have only to wait the arrival of all our purchases. Ah, here is Ned now."

The postilion drew the team to a halt before them and a footman assisted them inside. As they drove away, curses and yells from drivers and their masters mingled with the calls of venders, beggars, and waifs.

The abandoned children of London wrenched Joanne's heart, bringing to mind little Ellen and deepening her respect for Benjamin's work at Irwin Manor.

"You may not stop the coach," the comtesse said, taking Joanne's hand which was reaching to tap the glass before them.

"But they are so pitiful," Joanne said. The children's wretchedness reminded her of her own childhood as well.

"There are too many for you to care for," the comtesse said kindly. "Come," she chirped, "let us continue your study of the *ton*."

Resignedly Joanne looked out the closed windows and listened to her aunt's quips and informative descriptions of the men of "quality" who happened to pass them. "Lord Samuel, he shall be at the ball—we have already had his reply. Beware of him—he is famous for pinching unsuspecting females. Oh, my dear, look. It's Samuel Johnson and his friend Mr. Boswell. Lord Jason would enjoy visiting with them. Esspecially Johnson, after his pamphlet *Taxation No Tyranny* supporting the king. He certainly would be glad to know it has been a failure in convincing the people. I heard the other day that Johnson is returning to the literary field—writing an anthology of our poets, which should be accepted far better than his political writings. His *Dictionary* was such a success." A sudden, indrawn breath from her niece turned her head.

"Why, what is wrong?" she asked, seeing the chalk-white face of fear upon Joanne. She glanced quickly out the window and caught a glimpse of a straight-backed, harsh-faced man whipping his team through the jostling traffic. Taking the other's trembling hand in her own she asked, "Was it your father?"

Joanne nodded numbly.

"I wondered when we would chance upon him. His reply is also in—he is coming to the ball."

"No," begged Joanne.

"His invitation was from my own hand. He was asked to come as a favour to me, his dead wife's sister. We have never met—little does he suspect the surprise in store."

"I cannot go through with it," breathed Joanne.

"Can and will," clipped the comtesse.

Her sharp tone roused Joanne from her agitation. This tone from the gay, teasing comtesse?

"There are more people involved in this than you alone," sermonized her aunt. "You have my honour as well as your own to uphold. I cannot believe you will fall and mew at the man's feet like a whimpering kitten. Are you spineless? *La couard?*"

The answering glitter in Joanne's eyes eased the comtesse's sudden concern. The girl had to be free—to be happy, she had to face this.

"That is better. Now let us resume the lesson. Ah, there is Lord Humbolt—he would not make a bad husband. . . ."

Ames fidgeted in the seat, trying to wriggle into a tolerable position. He pushed at the side cushion, hoping to move some of the padding; his head stood in far greater need of it than his ribs. Settling as best he could, he looked across at his traveling companion through the rose-gray light of early dawn. Harrumphing mentally at the calm, relaxed features of the other, he closed his eyes. Sleep refused to come, despite his recent lack of it. Dr. Ames's thoughts turned to the cause of this mad, bone-rattling dash to London.

Returning to Kentoncombe the night of the departure of the two women, Ames had been greeted by a very distraught Mrs. Caern.

"Doctor, I am so glad you have come."

"What has happened?" he asked. Surely Kenton was not upset enough to . . . he did not complete the thought.

"Nothing . . . something . . . I don't know. What is one to make of it? After you left, his lordship ordered four bottles of his best port to be brought to his study. You know yourself his lordship isn't a drinking man—what did he need four bottles for?" Mrs. Caern's gesticulating and expression almost made Ames laugh. "Well, I asked why and nary a word would he speak—like a great stone he was."

"Did you have the wine brought?"

"What else could I do? No one disobeys Lord Jason. Out of sight he has stayed since I set those bottles on his desk. He thanked me politely—like he is, but there was that look. I had not seen it upon him since . . . since he ended mourning for his wife—God rest her soul. He won't answer when I knock or call and he has locked the door."

"Have you another key?"

In answer she pulled one from the oversized pocket of her crisp white apron.

Ames took it. "I will see to him." Hurried strides took him to the study door. "It is Ames, my lord." Putting his ear to the door, he heard no sound. The key clattered loudly to his ear as he turned it in the lock—the bolt thundered back. Ames pushed the door open.

"Why, Benjamin, how kind of you to come," Kenton greeted him softly, each word pronounced with minute care.

On the desk before Kenton, Ames saw the four bottles—three and a half now standing empty. "Good eve, my lord," he said, advancing slowly while he pondered what to do. "May I join you?"

"Would . . . you . . . care . . . for . . . a . . . glass . . . of . . . port?" In actions as slow and deliberate as his speech, Kenton reached for the half-empty bottle, poured some into a second goblet, and refilled his own. Not a drop was spilled.

Seating himself at the desk side, Ames marveled that Kenton was still conscious, much less lucid. For all appearances his lordship had just sat down for a glass of port. Only his studied speech and glassy expression betrayed the quantity he had imbibed.

"It is most sad, Benjamin," Kenton stated, staring ahead.

"What is, my lord?"

"That another should have her. And worse, you would have me go and witness it myself. I can be fool enough here."

With these words Kenton divulged the effect of the

wine, for he would never have said such under usual conditions. Curiosity prompted Ames to ask, "Why do you not woo her for yourself?"

"She thinks me too old—her father trusts me . . . could not betray that." Kenton leaned forward, gripping Ames's wrist. "You don't know what he did to her. He is worse than the renegade tomcat that devours its own young."

Ames drew back from the scathing contempt in the other's face. The tingling sensation in the wrist Kenton held turned his thoughts to himself. "You are right, my lord," he said soothingly while prying at Kenton's fingers with his free hand.

Releasing his grip, seemingly unaware that Ames had spoken or was trying to remove his hand, Kenton's features were weighted with sadness. "I dare not harm her further in an attempt to gain my happiness."

"Mayhap her feelings have changed," Ames said, taking advantage of Kenton's state to broach the subject so long straining to be voiced. "It is true she once believed she felt toward you as a daughter, but that was months past. Her feelings have changed. You must speak—she cannot broach it."

"So . . . sad," Kenton stated, making Ames realize he was too impaired by drink to understand.

Somehow he had managed to get Kenton abed and stayed the night, certain the man would be taken ill. In the morn Kenton did not have the grace to admit to even a headache. He asked Ames why he had stayed and apologized for any inconvenience in his usual calm, polite manner. Joanne's name was mentioned by neither then or any time until the letter from Furness.

Ames shifted in the golden velvet cushions again. Anything that looked so inviting had to have comfort somewhere within. To think he had despaired of Kenton's ever going to London. He thought back once more to that night of the three and a half port bottles, Kenton's one and only sign of distress. Through all the following days he had followed his normal routines as far as Ames could discern—with one added element. The time he would have spent with Joanne he now spent at Irwin Manor. The children welcomed his comings enthusiastically, for he always brought a treat—from sweets to rides in his open carriage. No one was left out or even forgotten, but one in particular did Kenton seek out. One in particular watched for his daily comings—Ellen. The other children recognized instinctively that the two had a special need for each other and were not jealous.

At times Kenton would take Ellen atop Asteron when he toured his renters' cottages or checked stock and crops. Mrs. Caern and Ames, the two persons now closest to him, found these days together eased the restless longing that showed only in his eyes when he thought he was unobserved.

Neither knew that when Kenton was with Ellen, away from everyone, he spoke of Joanne. The child gave empathy. Kenton, with no fear of her exposing his words, spoke freely.

Three days before he left for London he had called upon the child.

"You are looking well this morn, Miss Ellen." He made an elegant leg to the young child, who grabbed hold his neck as he did. "Happy to see me?" he asked, taking her up in his arms.

She nodded vigourously, then began going through his pockets. Finding the expected taffy, she hugged him and kissed his cheek before stuffing the candy into her mouth. "She is doing well, Benjamin." Kenton threw a smile at Ames who had joined them.

"Very well. Her colour is good, she eats well—but you can see that. No longer a stick of a child are you, Ellen?" he teased.

The little girl gurgled, covering her eyes shyly.

"Run along. Give this to Asteron," Kenton told Ellen, setting her down and giving her a piece of carrot. "I'll be right along."

"Her health is almost totally repaired," Ames answered the question before it was asked. "She now plays with the other children—takes hearty enjoyment in their games. But she has yet to speak. Let us hope this gurgling laughter which we hear from time to time means there is hope she shall one day speak.

"I never told Lady Joanne the extent to which the child had been abused—beaten almost to death before she was put in that basket on the hospital steps. Mayhap she only needs to learn to trust us enough to speak or mayhap she needs to have a great enough reason to break her silence." He began to add that the little girl had received a letter from Joanne but decided against it. "Ellen cares for you. One day she may speak for you."

Kenton nodded. "For her sake I hope so. I believe I'll not keep her out too long this day. There is a chill in the air." With a wave of his hand he strode toward Asteron. Tossing the little girl into the saddle, he gave the lad holding the reins a penny and mounted. "Would you like a gallop today?" he asked, settling in the saddle.

Her eager smile assured him and they were off.

Later, as they rode back toward Irwin, Kenton gave her a tight hug as she sat before him. "Do you miss Lady Joanne, Ellen? But I ask that every time, don't I?" he continued as she solemnly nodded. "I hope you don't miss her as I do." He stared straight ahead. "Remember the time she gave you the doll and you led me to her?" His voice choked as he recalled the feel of Joanne in his arms, the fragrance of her hair against his face.

Ellen turned and reached out, brushed his cheek as if wiping a tear away, then repeated the action upon her own cheek.

"What will we do, Ellen? I love her so." His voice quivered with the intensity of repressed feelings. *If only she were in my arms. God,* he thought, and looked away from the little girl's sorrowful stare, almost overcome.

Her hands reached up and tightened about his neck. A crooning sound came from her lips. As Joanne had sang to comfort her, Ellen now tried to comfort Kenton.

The days had passed uneventful since then and suddenly it was the day the comtesse had appointed for her ball.

Ames had walked into the study that afternoon unannounced, as had become his habit. Kenton was seated at his desk staring out the windows. The set of his shoulders, the veins extended along the side of his neck bespoke trouble. "Jason?" he said.

"I have heard from Furness," came the cold reply. "He demands his 'property' be shipped to London. He states that her future is settled."

"Then he does not know . . ."

"The comtesse has managed to keep the secret, but tonight it will be too late. I never should have agreed."

"But what can he do among so many? The comtesse is no fool—she will have taken measures."

"No woman is a match for Furness. Joanne is not safe. He must mean he has arranged a match—what devil has he bought for a husband?" Torture came through the words. "I leave for London in an hour—are you with me?"

"Arrangements must be made for my patients—the children," Ames sputtered, disconcerted at this unexpected turn.

"Then I go alone."

Ames disliked—distrusted the look upon Kenton's face; Furness would not be safe. "No, no, I can come. Let me fetch some clothing and speak with Dr. Fowler. I shall return within the hour—do not depart without me." He paused awaiting assurance.

"I shall not wait long—do not tarry."

So here I am, thought Ames, looking again at Kenton with a frown. Was this the man he meant to save from himself? From his demeanour one would think they were simply taking the children on a picnic—not trying to break the record time for reaching London . . . and the record for the number of bruises a man could have upon his ill-used body.

Chapter Eighteen

"Why, my dear Lord Furness," the vision of silk and lace said coyly.

His lordship haughtily took the hand held forth, brushing it lightly with his lips as he bowed. Straightening, he took in the comtesse's petite figure swathed in lilac silk, her tiny waist emphasized by the puffed skirt and low-cut stomacher. Swirls of gathered lace of a deeper hue decorated the skirt and sleeves and tiny embroidered shoes were just visible beneath the hem. The comtesse's powdered hair was dressed in elaborate curls, tucks of lace as in her gown adorning the work. She now took refuge behind the delicate lilac silk fan to hide her repugnance at his inspection.

"Dear sister," rolled from Furness's practiced tongue, "it is much to my regret that I did not know of your presence in London until now."

"It is as I wished—I have not been about much since my husband's death."

"Many will rejoice that you have ended your mourning."

"Only a cause so *dear* to *both* of us is responsible,

my lord." The comtesse arched her brows with implied meaning.

"Yes?" Furness responded, both puzzled and attracted.

"But, my lord, why do you feign no knowledge?" she asked.

Drawing the attention of those at the foot of the stairs on which they stood, the comtesse spoke loudly, "This is your proud moment, Lord Furness, and I only the humble servant." She twittered and fanned herself elaborately.

Gossiping among her guests ceased as they turned and strained to hear this conversation. Furness's reputation was well known and his presence a surprise for most of those invited. The comtesse, while not socializing widely, was known by many; few realized the relation between the two.

"*Messieurs, mesdames, et mesdemoiselles,*" the comtesse said, her eyes sweeping over the ballroom. "Few of you know that my sister was Lord Furness's wife."

Surprise showed on many—bafflement on Lord Furness.

"From their union was born a daughter." She smiled sweetly at Furness and was chilled by what she saw but continued. "It is with utmost pleasure that I have taken the child under my guidance for my poor brother and wish now to introduce her to all of you."

The comtesse and Furness were midway up the grand staircase that curved from the ballroom to the upper floor of private rooms, which was opened this eve so that the guests could refresh themselves and rest if they wished. At the top of the stairs now appeared a tall figure, the satin gown molded at the bodice and flowing widely from the back and waist in the popular sack style. The leaf-green colour was glossy against the flawless pink-hued skin of bust and arms. Tiny pink roses were scattered through the curls of the modest coiffure of white. The face resembled Furness's in looks, and the haughty cast and proud bearing were irrefutable proof of his kinship.

She met her father's eyes without wavering, taking the challenge, despite the fear pulsing through her. Slowly, grandly, she descended to within a step of the comtesse.

"Charming, is she not?"

The man stood in shock. A practiced gamester, his composure held and his looks did not betray the welter of feelings coursing through his veins. Never had he imagined . . . never.

"Will you do the honour of leading me in dance?" the comtesse asked, touching his arm lightly. "My guests await." A flick of her fan brought a dark-haired gentleman to their side. "You know Lord Humbolt, my lord. He has consented to lead Lady Joanne."

With a chilling smile and slight sneer, Furness bowed to the comtesse, conceding victory, and extended his hand. Leading her down the steps, he said softly, "I underestimated you, my lady."

"Thank you, my lord," she quipped in return.

"This eve shall not be forgotten. I owe you much," Furness continued. "And Lord Kenton as well."

As she looked up, the comtesse's brave spirit faltered —the devil himself could not have played the part better.

Joanne, for her part, felt her confidence grow as her father showed no overt reaction. Her fear had been for his temper—he had vent his spleen upon her too often for her not to be wary. Matching steps with Lord Humbolt, she even dared to think she might please her father.

Hope continued to flare anew as she glanced at the two leading the dance. The love she had sought so desperately—for which she had told herself repeatedly she had no need—seemed suddenly attainable. As with all creatures, the bond of parentage held fast in her; no matter what the past was, the longing to be loved existed still.

The discipline that Kenton had instilled and the comtesse had refined held Joanne in good stead when, at the close of the first set, she and the comtesse changed partners. Furness said nothing as he stood before her, waiting for the music to begin. Neither approval nor disapproval showed, only the familiar masked coldness. As he did not speak, she also did not.

As the dance ended, he bowed over her hand and kissed it lightly. Her heart thrilled—her father had never touched her kindly before—only to be plummeted to the depths by the look of hatred that flared, then was hidden as he straightened. "Your mother would be pleased," he said icily, not looking at her as she allowed him to place her hand upon his arm.

When another claimed Joanne for the next country set, she blushed as Furness noted with undue volume, "I shall not have a daughter long—marry she will." His eyes bored into hers and she sensed a threat. "And soon," he added.

Through the rest of the night Joanne's mind went over and over those words—the only words he had spoken directly to her. What did they mean?

Many drawn to meet Joanne during the eve, attracted by her father's reputation, were charmed by the serious daughter so unlike him. Remembrances of her haughtiness were broken by the charm of her smile.

Lack of the frivolity and shyness that most green girls had in excess was an asset for Joanne. Her education and wide reading made her an interesting conversationalist and as the week passed she grew to be a favourite for sensible chats among old and young alike. Under the tutelage of the comtesse, Joanne managed a few skills of the flirt but, despite her aunt's encouragement and example, she used them rarely.

The days passed in morning calls, afternoons in the park, evenings at the various assemblies. The comtesse and Lord Furness's daughter became a popular sight and were sought after by small and grand hostesses alike.

If any noted the lack of attention Furness paid his daughter, few gave it any importance. If anything, she was aided by his absence. His intimates, surprised to find his lordship with so comely a daughter after having seen Joanne at Furness House, learned quickly not to speak of her in his presence.

"Must we go?" Joanne asked petulantly. "I am exhausted. Could we not stay home this one eve?"

"Nonsense," laughed the comtesse. "I had quite forgotten the social whirl. Think, there are eight weeks more. Do you not delight in being surrounded—sought after?" She patted a powdered curl in place. "It brings to mind the gay days in Paris." The cast of sadness that swooped upon her was repelled determinedly.

"We have just begun and must make the best use of all this attention. The *ton* is fickle. Even Richard Sheridan has been complimentary of your looks and that is a fête on your part, for the poor man is being harried to death to finish his latest work. I hear it is to be entitled 'The School for Scandal.'" She studied Joanne for a moment and pouted, "You do not find that *intéressant*? Do you not know how fortunate you are to take such a man's notice? Have you found none attractive?"

Shrugging, Joanne turned to her mirror. "There are those who could be termed handsome, but they lack a . . . a maturity. Those that have age lack . . . looks."

The comtesse smiled knowingly. "I see . . . You find none that interest you as a husband?"

A blush crept over Joanne's cheeks as she thought of Jason.

"Ah, then there is someone. But I shall not be a tease." The comtesse patted her niece's hand. "Hurry —I do not wish to arrive too late. Lord Perton has promised I shall find the night interesting," she winked. "Let us hope he is correct." Her tinkling laugh followed her from the room.

I never know how to take her words, thought Joanne. *She is ever joyful and yet a sense of subdued sorrow seems to hover behind all the gaiety.* Did the comtesse long for someone, for . . . Kenton? The name came unbidden.

Angrily Joanne threw open her closet doors and grabbed a wild-rose-colored gown—the most daring of those she had gotten, being very décolleté. She held it against her now slender form and looked into her mirror. "If only I could leave my hair unpowdered," she said, thinking how her dark hair would be highlighted by the satin's glow. Suddenly she saw as plainly as if he were truly there Kenton smiling over her shoulder. She could tell the touch of his hands upon her shoulders. Then his features faded. "You must stop thinking of him," she scolded herself. Laying the dress across the settee in her room, she sat before the mirror and began applying the light makeup the comtesse had given her.

How did I ever imagine I loved him as a father, she thought as she rubbed the lightest tinge of red across her lips. Her blood surged as she thought of Kenton, so tall, so handsome, so quietly strong. She thought of his passionate gaze that day he had stood outside her bedroom door and now she cursed her failure to recognize its meaning. Joanne shook herself. It would not do, she told herself. He did not love her or he would never have allowed her to leave.

Lord Humbolt bowed over Joanne's hand. "May I fetch you something to drink?" he asked. Even early in the season the heat of the multitude of candles lighting the Mortons' ballroom and the crush of the crowd was taking its toll.

"Champagne, please," Joanne responded. Thinking of Kenton had made her reckless.

The comtesse hovered several paces away. She had curtailed her own flirting to keep watch over her suddenly coquettish niece. Was it only five days ago that she had introduced Joanne to society? A tallish man sidled up to Joanne. *I know him, oui,* the comtesse thought. *He is Lord Wiltham—there is something* displeasing about him. She was certain Humbolt had just gone to fetch something to drink and here Wiltham was giving Joanne champagne. He was not to be trusted—no gentleman this. Her friends might know something of the man.

"My lady."

Turning, the comtesse was greeted by Furness's wicked smile.

"I see your charge is doing well. She could choose worse."

"You know Lord Wiltham, my lord?" she questioned.

"Vaguely."

"That, at least, is to Wiltham's credit," the comtesse said. "I wonder that the entertainment here is not too *domestiqué* for your taste, my lord."

"Would you have me take my duty as a father lightly?" he asked, only his eyes betraying his true feelings. "I must see how my daughter progresses. I would not like to be embarrassed by any untoward behaviour on her part."

"Behaviour such as your own, my lord?" the comtesse asked, a light smile failing to disguise the sarcasm.

"You would be wise to tread lightly," Furness answered, his smile matching her own. He bowed nobly and sauntered away.

Tapping her foot furiously, the comtesse contemplated Furness's back, then swung her eyes to where Joanne and Wiltham stood. Her niece laughed at something he said, then boldly handed Humbolt her glass and went with Wiltham to join the dancers. A lecture was in order.

"You are most beautiful," a voice she knew said behind the comtesse.

A relieved smile came upon her; her spirit soared. "Lord Kenton," she said, turning and heartily embracing the startled man.

The name came to Joanne's ears even across the room. She saw the happiness upon the comtesse's face and noted with everyone else the warmth of the greeting.

"Ah, Dr. Ames," the comtesse greeted the doctor standing behind Kenton. "I am happy to see you also."

"And I you," he returned.

"Is all well?" Kenton asked urgently, keeping hold of her hand.

"Of course, my lord. But why would it not be?" She followed Kenton's eyes to where Joanne stood, now flirting outrageously with Wiltham. "You see she has adapted to London's ways."

"Who chose that gown?" Kenton demanded, not hearing the comtesse. "It is indecent."

"Indecent, my lord?" teased the comtesse. "Indeed, I can assure you the gentlemen have been most generous with compliments."

The muscles along Kenton's jaw line flexed visibly and the comtesse was hard put to restrain herself. "But this is a surprise. Do you come on business? Will you be able to stay long?" she asked, turning to a less tempting subject.

"I decided a time away from his duties would benefit Dr. Ames and also I have some business matters to attend to. A leisurely journey is always relaxing," Kenton said casually.

Ames choked on the champagne he had begun to drink.

"Are you all right?" the comtesse asked, fluttering to his side.

"Yes, my lady," Ames coughed out. "Merely a misswallow." He looked at Kenton, but the other was again watching Joanne. *Leisurely journey indeed!* thought Ames. Even a broken axle had added only one day to it. Why, they had arrived only hours ago. The bed at their rental lodgings had been most inviting, but Kenton had demanded that they dress and off they had gone to the comtesse's, then on to here when they had learned her direction for the evening.

"Is it as we believed?" the comtesse whispered to Ames.

The doctor nodded, a wide smile erasing the tired lines from his face.

"Then let us drink," she said, taking Ames's glass and replacing it with another from a passing footman's tray. "To the future."

Both drank, but Ames was at a loss—Lady Joanne appeared most content with her escort and Kenton's masked features gave little hope.

Chapter Nineteen

"What do you mean your mistress is not at home?" snapped Kenton.

"Easy, man," prodded Ames. Their eyes locked and slowly the glare eased.

"Can you tell me where they have gone?"

"No, *monsieur*."

"Which direction did their carriage take?" Kenton asked, desperate for any hint.

The small butler shrugged, easing the door shut. *These English,* he thought. This one does not give up easily—morning calls, messages left, and now returning in the evening, but it was not his place to question the comtesse's orders.

"Let us return to our rooms," Ames urged.

"No, we shall go to each assembly we have a card to. They must be at one of them."

"But they could just as easily have gone to Hay Market, Drury Lane, or even to Ranelagh or Vauxhall," Ames told him tiredly. "What is the use? We have come too oft as it is. You left word that we would call this eve. The comtesse would see us if she

wished to. May is already here—June could come before we tracked them down."

"Come, Benjamin, it is not that bad. Have you not
enjoyed seeing so much of London since we arrived?"

"See it is all I have been able to do—I would like
to enjoy it also," Ames responded, his temper irked
to the limit.

"I dare say we have dashed about a bit," Kenton
answered.

"Oh you do, my lord. There are other words I would
choose but, as my station in life warrants it, I bow to
yours. Now I am going back to our rooms—will you
come?"

"No, I believe I will take in Ranelagh, but do not
let that forestall you."

At a loss to understand Kenton, Ames shrugged
and signaled a sedan chair. The man has changed
from a sane, rational being to a dashed idiot, he
thought. So much for the power of love.

"My terms have not altered."

"But my lord, I could woo and wed her willingly . . ."

"You fail to understand, Wiltham." The hard eyes
bore through him. "The key to our agreement is that
your bride will be kept at Wornstone. I care not if
she lives or dies there but I wish neither to see nor
hear of her presence elsewhere."

"It cannot be done, my lord. Times have changed.
. . . Lady Joanne is comely—why this aversion on . . ."

"You are forgetful, are you not?" The fiery tone
halted Wiltham's words. "Will you sacrifice your

home, your livelihood, your honour for a pretty wench?"

Wiltham whitened under the worded threat. "My lord, she is your daughter, I . . ."

"Your kind snivels about honour," sneered Furness, "but care not how it is maintained. Listen well—gainsay you are with me in this." No words came from the whipped figure. "As I thought. Then we proceed. You have done well as far as it goes. Many have noted your company with my daughter, and her liking of it. This Friday next there is to be a masque at Ranelagh. See to it that Joanne attends this. Her current rebellious mood should make it easier for you.

"Once at Ranelagh you shall take her into the gardens. Men will be waiting for you at a fixed point— the rest should be perfectly clear," he paused and the other nodded. "A coach and four will be waiting to bring you here. I have found an elderly cleric that will do my bidding in the matter. Once wed, you will be off to Wornstone. What you do from there is for you to decide." The voice hardened. "Breaking our agreement, however, will cause you to forfeit all present and future sums. Be true to the bargain, though, and you shall have all that is not entailed when I die."

A surge of greed overwhelmed whatever compassion Wiltham had felt. Lady Joanne's feelings were not worth a fortune and what could be purchased with it. *She's as proud as this devil,* Wiltham thought. *There could be much pleasure in taming her.* "It will be as you say, my lord," he agreed, "but what of the comtesse?"

"When you are safely away, I shall call upon her

myself to deliver the happy tidings. Who will question what I say?" Gloating confidence lit his features in a devilish smile.

The feeling was conveyed to Wiltham and he drew his own importance from it. "The papers for the . . ."

"Will be signed when you and Joanne arrive at my lodgings," Furness stated curtly. "Now, should you not be elsewhere, wooing your *love*?"

Snide laughter barked from the younger man. "Ah, yes," Wiltham said, taking up Furness's spirit. "Off to Ranelagh. Lord Perton was to include the comtesse and Lady Joanne in his party this eve."

Furness sat brooding in his chair after Wiltham's departure. His wife's features appeared dimly before his eyes. He quaffed the glass of port in his hand, savouring the warmth of the liquid, its balm soothing his conscience. "I must follow the path I have begun," he muttered aloud. Not to do so would . . . He tossed the thought aside and refilled his glass. Unrelenting pain of loss, of his inability to prevent his wife's death, these had turned to hatred for his infant daughter. Hatred had twisted his pride and made him unrelenting. Through the years it had become his habit to abuse her and to drown his conscience in drink and raucous activity. To admit he might have been wrong all these years was impossible.

Concerned over the comtesse's fretting about Joanne, Lord Perton had convinced her that a night at Ranelagh strolling to the music of the orchestra was just the antidote needed. A party was arranged to include Lord Humbolt and his cousin, Lady Sarah, who were friends of Lord Perton, along with Sir Blyme, his wife, and a Mr. Rogers.

Arriving at the gardens by coach, the party paid their half crowns and proceeded through the dimly lit paths. Suddenly the Rotunda loomed before them, its circular frame bathed in light. All except Joanne had been there before and she was delighted with the tall roundness of the structure, so vastly different from every other she had seen. According to the comtesse, Dr. Johnson had called it the finest thing he had ever seen.

Inside, the vast blue ceiling reflected the shadows of those promenading beneath it. The circular walls were lined with gaily painted and decorated refreshment stands for those who wished to partake. In the center, inside ornate columns and banisters, an orchestra played. Chandeliers glowing with a multitude of candle flames flickered above the slowly parading beaux and elegantly gowned ladies, while ordinary people mingled among the luxuriously dressed. Anyone with the price of admission could enter and ogle the flaunted wealth.

Agog at the sights, Joanne, on Lord Humbolt's arm, followed her aunt and Perton. About them ranged the other members.

"Does this place please you?" Humbolt asked, seeking to break Joanne's silence.

"What, my lord? Oh, of course. Never have I seen the like. So many people, such a . . . varied gathering and so elegant." She spoke no more, busy absorbing the sights all about her.

Men in immense periwigs and women in intricate,

powdered coiffures were parading in the slowly revolving crowd beneath the Rotunda. The heavy make-up on many of the men as well as the outrageous dress of several of the women came as a surprise. Light powder, perhaps a patch or two, she had noticed on some during her weeks in London, but nothing had prepared her for the sights here. The nobility, the gentry, the common—high- and lowbred mingled. The clothing on most was expensive, but it seemed to Joanne, overhearing the conversation of those who passed by, that the more expensive the clothes, the more guttural the language. With relief she followed Lord Perton toward their box.

Halfway to the box, Lord Kenton joined the party. The comtesse graciously introduced him to all. She allowed no more than polite exchanges, however, before exclaiming, "You must forgive us, Lord Kenton, but we are about to partake of the refreshments—the evening air can parch a throat so. So nice to see you. Do call upon us soon," she added archly, knowing full well it was her contrivance that had caused Kenton and Ames to miss them no matter when they called. With the poise of a general she mustered the party off before he could ask to join them.

Kenton's tall figure, left standing alone among the slowly circling walkers, attracted a courtesan's attention. Fan aflutter, she paused and nodded at him before swaying past. Observing her, his thoughts went to Joanne; she had looked tired. Had she missed his company? Gazing at the box in which she sat, he saw that she was now leaning against Humbolt's arm, enjoying something he had said. Kenton's eyes went back to the courtesan's inviting figure. If Joanne could enjoy herself, so could he.

A few quick steps brought him apace with the heavily rouged woman. He found her quite willing to dispense with a formal introduction by a third party. No time was lost in settling into a smaller booth not far from Joanne and the comtesse.

When the courtesan flung herself upon Kenton's lap, Joanne increased her impromptu flirting. *So this was the serious man from Kentoncombe,* she thought. She would show him how little she cared.

The result was that Lord Humbolt was embarrassed, the comtesse angered, Sir Blyme and his wife offended, and Joanne no less mollified. When Wiltham came upon the scene, he was appreciative. It took little effort to win Joanne's consent to walk in the gardens with him, something a proper young lady would never have done.

The garrishly bejeweled damsel upon Kenton's lap found herself deposited solidly upon a chair, coin laid upon the table more than ample for the charges incurred, and a farewell said with more speed than their meeting had required. She made a face as she watched him pursue the pair from the other box, then dropped the coins into her bodice and went seeking more promising game.

The bright lights about the Rotunda dimmed swiftly on the garden paths. Her lack of wisdom in agreeing to walk alone with Wiltham smote Joanne as raucous laughter lifted from the hidden arbours in the gardens. "I wish to return to my aunt," she said to him, uneasy of the hold he maintained upon her arm.

"We have just left them. The air is so refreshing

here. Do not hang back—are you frightened of me?" he asked, his hold tightening.

"Of course not. I simply wish to return to the others. It was not polite of me to leave as I did."

"What? With Furness blood in your veins I should think you would care little about others."

"My lord." Joanne halted. "I will thank you to release my arm. I am turning back."

"I have no intention of . . ."

"My lady," Kenton said, silently stepping to Joanne's side. "May I be of service?"

"You have not been invited to join us—whoever you are," Wiltham sneered.

"I am not speaking to you," Kenton cut him, taking hold of Joanne's free arm.

"Do you know this . . . person?" Wiltham asked her, weighing what to do.

"Yes. An old . . . friend. Lord Kenton, this is Lord Wiltham. Would you escort me back to the comtesse?" she asked Kenton, trying to read his expression in the dim light.

Not daring to cause a scene, Wiltham fumed but released his hold and made a leg. Certainty that he would have his way with Joanne in the end caused him to smile. "I apologize, Lord Kenton—didn't know you were acquainted with Lady Joanne. Mustn't be too careful." Kenton's scowl turned Wiltham's self-confidence sour.

Joanne and Kenton walked back to the box inside the Rotunda in silence. Joanne longed to move her arm from Kenton's grasp and take hold his hand, but his stiff walk and ill-concealed disapproval restrained her from such wanton behaviour.

Kenton himself was struggling to hold back the sermon he was wont to give her. As they neared the box, he halted a few steps from the others, having caught the comtesse's eye and nodding to show all was well. "My lady," was all he said as he bowed over Joanne's hand before turning on heel and departing.

The two brief words echoed over and over as she watched his steady progress through the parade of strollers.

Oh, reprimand most dearly remembered, she thought. Could it be—could he be jealous or was her heart grasping at a foolish hope?

Foolish indeed, she told herself, realizing Jason would never speak. The fear of rejection, a fear strongly fortified by her father's treatment, forestalled any chance of her broaching the subject.

Chapter Twenty

Wiltham's ill-humour, begun by Kenton's interruption in the Ranelagh gardens and fed by his own inflated ego, flared when Furness joined him in a private room at a gaming house not frequented by their acquaintances. Three bottles of port had fortified his bravado. "If it were not for the import of what you would have me do, I would duel with the man," he snarled as Furness helped himself to the bottle of port upon the table. "Confound him—you know the man," he said to Furness as a long-forgotten conversation returned to him.

"Of whom are you speaking—you make no sense," the irritated man snapped.

"Why, Lord Kenton."

"Why do you speak of him?" Furness's eyes narrowed as he awaited the reply.

"I was walking with Lady Joanne in the gardens at Ranelagh when he intervened. Your daughter seemed uncommonly friendly with him. I . . ."

"Fool," snarled Furness, grabbing Wiltham by the

stock about his neck. "Have you destroyed all chance of luring her there on Friday next?"

"No, my lord." Wiltham clawed at Furness's hand. "It is merely that your daughter wished to return to the Rotunda and I . . ."

"There is only one reason a man beguiles a woman to the dark walks at Ranelagh—I had not thought you so stupid!" Another thought interrupted Furness, for his facial features suddenly relaxed and he released his hold. A malevolent laugh come from deep in his throat. "You say she was partial to Kenton?"

"I do not think that, my lord. She was perhaps, perhaps not. *Certe,* he is not taken with her, for I saw him leave the Rotunda as quickly as he entered it," whined Wiltham.

His last words were not heard. "So her punishment is to be doubled, is it," he said to himself. Gremlins seemed to dance in his eyes as he ordered, "Be certain you amend any ill feeling my daughter may have toward you."

"Ill feeling? Of course she has none. . . ."

"Do not bother with your words—I know you too well to be fobbed off. I warn you though, save any further ardour till you are wed. It is, after all, only six days hence."

Saturday and Sunday passed with the tension between aunt and niece unalleviated. The comtesse's concern over Joanne and the worry that she had carried her strategy with Kenton too far, since he had not called since Friday eve, showed on her face as she entered Joanne's chamber on Monday evening.

"What a serious face you have, Aunt," Joanne noted

lightly. "Has Lord Perton sent word he will not be at the soirée?"

"If that was all I have to be disturbed about, my heart would be light," she rejoined. Her features softened. "We must speak, Joanne," the comtesse began.

"But I must finish dressing," Joanne returned, sensing the lecture she had been expecting for days.

"It will not matter if we are late. Please, look at me and listen."

A frown creased Joanne's forehead as she turned and looked to her aunt.

"I have said very little about your behaviour, for I know you are neither accustomed to the city's ways nor have you had opportunities to enjoy yourself. But I cannot tolerate your irresponsible behaviour with Lord Humbolt."

"Humbolt," burst from Joanne, certain that her aunt was speaking of Wiltham. "But I have done nothing . . ."

"You have been the proper miss one moment with that poor young man and an outlandish coquette the next instant. I shall not even mention your behaviour with Lord Wiltham—I believe you know how disgraceful that has been."

"I am truly sorry for that, Aunt. It will not happen again, I assure you, and I promise to be most ladylike with Lord Humbolt from now on."

"You have no idea the impression you give with such vacillating moods. If Lord Kenton had not brought you back to our box at Ranelagh the other night . . . well, I shudder to think of the consequences."

"A walk in the gardens cannot ruin a reputation," Joanne returned, her anger growing. Kenton's name was fuel to the smoldering embers; for all his evident concern he had not called since.

"You have forgotten that you have to live down your father's reputation first. Everyone watches to see if you will be of his kind." The comtesse stepped closer. Uncharacteristically, she bit her lip, then asked, "Can you not . . . confide in me? There must be a reason behind your changeable conduct. Could it be that you wish to make someone jealous?"

The to then unrealized truth touched home. Colour faded from Joanne's cheeks. "Just because you act thusly with Perton to make Kenton jealous is no reason to accuse me," she threw back defensively.

The comtesse reeled. Is this what the child thought; no wonder her shifting demeanour. "No, no, Joanne. You are wrong. I care nothing for Lord Kenton—he is but a friend," she hastened to say.

The speed of the rebuttal only confirmed Joanne's belief. She rose haughtily, barely in control. *Let them have one another*, she thought. *I owe them happiness, even if it breaks my heart*. "I must dress, Aunt. I give my word to bring no further dishonour upon you—is that satisfactory?"

"That is nonsense," the comtesse said, restraining the urge to slap some sense into the silly child. "What do I care of honour? Let me help you," she begged, trying to reach across the barrier Joanne was erecting.

Deaf to the plea, Joanne went to her seat before her vanity table and began powdering her face.

The comtesse gazed at her sadly but there was little she could do now. Perhaps if she spoke to Kenton . . . *How foolish I was to think I was handling this so well,* she thought sadly. Now to right things before it is too late. But how, with two as stubborn as she knew these to be.

Nothing changed between the two as they traveled to Devonshire house for the duchess's ball. In an effort to ease the tension, the comtesse noted, "We are very fortunate to have been invited—many would do anything for an invitation from the duchess. It is said only the best of society are invited."

"Then I should not have been," snapped Joanne, instantly regretting her words as their effect showed on her aunt's face.

"Ma chère nièce," the comtesse breathed, "do not be so."

"Please, Aunt," Joanne began then paused. "Let us do as you oft say," she continued with feigned lightheartedness, "and enjoy ourselves. No more sad thoughts."

Their conversation turned to fashion and gossip from past days as they waited patiently for their coach to reach the front of the long lines of coaches converging on Devonshire House. This became strained and silence fell as they reached the head of the line and were released from their coach and escorted to the ballroom.

One of the first to greet them was Lady Sarah, Humbolt's cousin, who had been with them at Ranelagh. She drew Joanne to one side when one of the dowagers present commanded the comtesse's attention. "Have you heard there is to be a masquerade?" she whispered excitedly.

"A masque—but where, when?" Joanne asked.

"At Ranelagh on Friday eve," Lady Sarah returned. "Would you like to go?"

"But at Ranelagh . . ." Joanne hesitated.

"Do not pretend to be innocent," Sarah responded tartly, glancing about to see if anyone was listening.

"I . . . I have to ask Aunt."

"Do not do that," Sarah exclaimed in a whisper. "Why she will only say it is not the thing for young ladies."

"Then I must not go. I have just promised Aunt I would do better. How could we go if I do not ask?" questioned Joanne, sensing there was more intent to Sarah's question than gaining mere knowledge.

"Walk with me," Sarah said, putting her arm through Joanne's. "I was thinking I could talk Cousin Humbolt into taking us if you would agree to come. Oh, say you will. I so long to go to a masquerade. We could leave long before the unmasking—no one need know we had gone."

"I don't know . . ."

"I will be forever in your debt," pleaded Lady Sarah, "if only you will come."

Looking at the imploring face, Joanne was loath to disappoint one so eager. "I shall speak to the comtesse about it," she said finally.

"That will never do—she will only refuse and then watch you closely so there will be no chance of our going," the other wailed.

"What is this you speak of?" chimed in the comtesse's voice from behind.

Both girls started guiltily.

"Come, come—what was it you were saying you wanted to do?" she asked encouragingly.

"It is only . . . only that we would like to go to the masquerade at Ranelagh, Aunt," Joanne said. "Lord Humbolt would be willing to escort us," she added quickly.

Recalling her own youth, the older woman smiled at the younger two. "I believe we may go—if we plan on departing early," she answered to their surprise. "Let us ask Lord Kenton and Dr. Ames also—we have neglected them sadly since their arrival."

"Thank you, oh, thank you, my lady," breathed Lady Sarah happily.

The comtesse's laughter tinkled gaily at Sarah's excitement. "Ah," she said, signaling the two with her fan, "partners for the dance approach."

Hurried strides brought Wiltham to Joanne's side just ahead of Humbolt. There was no choice but to accept his hand or deal with a scene. Joanne treated him coldly throughout the steps. When the music ended, he bowed and offered, "I most humbly implore your forgiveness, my lady. My behaviour at Ranelagh was beyond bounds."

"There is nothing to forgive, my lord," Joanne returned coolly, looking over the crowd.

"But I wish to make amends," continued Wiltham. "Surely you know I regard you in a much different light than friend—alone. I would be downcast if you were to hold me in disfavour. Could I not escort you and your aunt to the masque on Friday?"

"We have already made our plans," Joanne answered. She could see Kenton's head, bent as if listening to someone—those moving about him concealed to whom.

"Then I shall see you there?" Wiltham asked nervously.

A wave of her hand and an irritated nod signaled yes.

Relief flooded over Wiltham's features. "It will be delightful to see you there then. What shall you be wearing?"

Focusing her attention back to him, Joanne thought to be rid of him. "I would think my yellow gown—it will contrast well with my black domino."

Claimed for the next dance by Humbolt, she got a better view of those standing about the sides. It struck her odd that Lady Sarah was speaking urgently with Wiltham—she had not thought them known to one another. What could they be about? The sight of the comtesse and Kenton in the group just ahead distracted her. So that was who he had been speaking with. Her resolve was strengthened—these two were the only ones who had shown her any love. Since Kenton cared nothing for her, the least she could do was see to it that the comtesse snared him.

"Are you troubled, my lady?" Kenton asked the comtesse as the last step was taken and they rose from their respective bow and curtsy. "Your smile is not as frequent as it should be."

"Perhaps I am tired," she tossed back. "Now you must assure me that I am forgiven and that you and Benjamin will escort my party to Ranelagh for the masque."

"I had thought our company was not desired," he returned archly.

"Why, Lord Kenton, you are becoming a flirt."

"An art others practice well," he noted.

"But there is always a reason for it. Perhaps the one you speak of wishes to make another jealous."

"Jealous?"

"Are you such a stranger to women's ways?" She laughed and put her arm about his. "Let us get something cool and refreshing while I educate *you,* my lord."

Chapter Twenty-one

During his stay with Lord Kenton in London, Dr. Ames had been sorely tried in many ways, but never had he had to wait upon his lordship to complete his toilet—in fact, the opposite had oft been true. Therefore on the night of the masque, Ames began early and with pointed self-satisfaction appeared at Kenton's door.

His lordship was having some difficulty deciding what to wear and Ames first stood to one side offering suggestions. Then he leaned against the carved bedpost and watched, his illusion of Kenton as a faultless and rapid dresser dispelled. Now he was sitting—his lordship's stock causing the current delay—contemplating whether or not he should lie upon his lordship's bed. "My lord," he ventured, looking at the pitiful scene of a man in love striving to dress, "would it be ungallant of me to mention that your domino will cover almost all of what you have laboured over."

Kenton flung an unappreciative frown at Ames.

"We are already late." Ames rose carelessly. "Should I send a message that . . ."

"Your words are well noted, Benjamin. I am finished." With a last glimpse at his finely-knitted fawn-coloured breeches, a tug at the fawn waistcoat covered with embroidery in shades of rust, a shrug to test the fit of his rust evening coat, and an adjustment to his cream-coloured stock, he left his mirror. Picking up the black domino, Kenton paused. "Do you suppose I should have gotten a domino of different colour?"

Ames's look of disbelief was sufficient answer.

A like scene was being played at the comtesse's. While Joanne's interest in her appearance had increased greatly since coming to London, it was her aunt who usually found fault with it. This eve, however, Joanne had already changed gowns five times. The comtesse entered just as the fifth gown was being removed.

"Surely you are not going to change again?" she asked, hidden laughter sparkling through her words.

"It just does not suit. What am I to do?" Joanne asked plaintively.

"I believe the first—the bright sunshine yellow—was the best selection," her aunt answered. "Why not put it on and *not* look in the mirror. That is the only cure for such indecision. After all, the domino will cover all but the skirt.

"But hurry now. Lord Kenton is past due already and it would never suit him to be kept waiting."

"I cannot see why Lord Humbolt and Lady Sarah could not ride with us," Joanne commented as she was helped once again into the yellow gown.

"I have explained it. Lord Kenton's coach is too small for three gowns held out by panniers *and* three gentlemen. It would not have been polite to suggest he find a larger one.

"Now we are quite familiar with Lord Kenton and Dr. Ames. Do you not desire some time to speak with them without others about?" the comtesse baited.

"Certainly I am pleased to be able to visit with Benjamin," Joanne returned, thinking how difficult it would be to bear having to see Kenton alone without the diversion of others.

"Why the frown?" questioned her aunt. "Afraid Lord Humbolt will choose not to come?"

"What? Oh, no. I am quite certain he will bring Sarah. So should you be," she tossed a puzzled glance at the comtesse, "for it was you who asked if he would mind going separately."

"Right you are. There, the gown is fastened. Now, gather your gloves, reticule—don't forget your fan; it will be beastly warm," the comtesse called as she moved lightly to the door. "And do not forget to bring your domino."

"Good eve, Benjamin, Lord Jason," the comtesse greeted the men as they entered her drawing room. She saw Kenton's eyes fasten on Joanne, who refused to look at him. "Come, come, everyone," she chattered, bustling about, hurrying all to the waiting coach. "Benjamin, how elegant you look this eve. You must sit beside me," she told him with a wink as they stepped out into the street.

"The comtesse is very lovely tonight," Joanne said

to Kenton, attempting to put her good intention to work.

"I suppose she is," came tactlessly from Jason who found Joanne irresistibly beautiful this eve. "You . . . you are . . . in good looks." He stumbled over the words, his tongue refusing to cooperate.

How tall, how elegant he is, Joanne thought, *the handsomest of men.*

"Are you going to stay in the street?" prompted the comtesse as the pair stood at the door gazing at each other.

Kenton started. "Your hand, my lady," he offered.

Laying her hand in his firm, warm hold, Joanne drew her breath in sharply and hastened to step up into the coach. His touch was as a spark to the dry straw of her heart. Sitting, she met her aunt's curious look and a choking tightness came over her.

In the street Kenton hesitated, the desire to stalk away strong upon him. Could he be so close to his love, have her beauty so near and not take her in his arms, not kiss the frown now upon her brow away? He took a deep breath, bidding his heart be still. Tell her how ravishing she is, it insisted, but an unfamiliar awkwardness seized him. He sat, catching part of her gown, then rose, thumping his head against the coach's roof, and was in an emotional shambles by the time her skirt was free and both seated again.

Beside him, suffering similarly, Joanne did not notice Kenton's sudden ineptness. The pulse beating within yearned for his arm to be close about her, for those brown eyes staring so resolutely ahead to look at her full of love. Joanne snapped her fan open. It would never do to wonder how the touch of his lips would feel when she thrilled so at a mere touch of his hand. I cannot endure this, she thought, fanning herself distractedly. I must not think. He loves the comtesse. Suddenly tears welled. Behind her fan she rubbed one from the corner of her eye, thankful for the darkness.

"Ellen is doing well," Kenton blurted, his mind finally finding a subject. "She has missed you." He looked at Joanne. *God, how I have missed you,* he thought.

"I have oft had her in my thoughts—have written her because of it," Joanne said, glancing at his profile. *And thought about you,* she added in her thoughts. "Has she ever spoken?" she asked, a fear entering her heart. Perhaps Jason was so cold to her because Ellen had spoken—had told him all she had said of her love for him. It had been easy to speak of that love to the little foundling. If only Jason could love her as Ellen did.

"No, she has not." He thought of his last visit with Ellen, how she had run to hug him, how he had seen her run to hug Joanne so oft in the past. Joanne loved the blue-eyed waif. If she could but love him a little as well.

Desultory conversation ensued as the two battled to control their emotions—control the desire that flamed afresh at each brush of their arms, at each glance.

Beside them the comtesse was revived; her gay spirit soared. With the two at last together, acting just as two people in love ought to act, the matter was definitely looking more promising. What she had in mind for this eve should open the way for a marriage announcement on the morrow—perhaps later, she conceded, considering Kenton's penchant for being proper.

Content to let them struggle with the conversation, she thought placidly of weddings and happier days, never realizing how close marriage actually hovered.

The streets they traveled were filled with people—elegantly gowned ladies with plumes and jewels, silver-buckle-shod gentlemen with powder and patch, inconspicuous pickpockets with quicksilver fingers, and the ordinary folk with eyes eager for all. Nearing the entrance of Ranelagh, their coach was slowed by the force of the throng as many were gathered in clusters, hawking flowers, ogling, and harassing those entering.

"We had better put on our dominos," the comtesse chirped to Joanne, "or we shall have little chance of concealing our identities.

"Lord Kenton, please assist Joanne—it is quite impossible to put the mask on without crushing one's hair." She handed Ames hers as if to prove the necessity.

Timidly Joanne held her mask out to Kenton. He took it, glancing to see how Ames was managing, and shrugged. Both women were wearing wide hoop panniers to hold out their full skirts; sitting beside them was in itself a struggle.

Realizing Kenton was stymied, the comtesse suggested, "Joanne, if you turn your back to Lord Kenton, matters will be much simplified."

Unusually biddable, Joanne managed the pannier enough to turn. His lordship reached out; their hands touched as Joanne reached up to position the mask—

pulses leaped in response. His heart pounding awry, Kenton managed to tie the mask. Taking the hooded cloak, his hands brushed across her shoulders.

Impulses to laugh, to scream, to cry raged in Joanne. His very touch inflamed her. It was a torture difficult to endure, knowing she would never be held in his arms.

In relief, both settled back in place. Each sought to recall their resolves: Joanne to try and aid the comtesse, Kenton not to give vent to his feelings.

The resolutions were promptly weakened as Kenton handed Joanne out of the coach. The high spirits of those milling about them made it evident that the men would have to shield the ladies from the bolder sallies. As Ames had somehow managed to have his arm about the comtesse, Kenton could only turn to Joanne. She misconstrued his reluctance and bit her lip to stay the threatening tears as his arm settled protectively about her.

He guided her forward, relishing her nearness. The crowd jostled them, throwing them together. *How can she not see my love,* he thought, as Joanne clung to his arm. The mob pushed them on in a sea of motion. Even after entering the safety of the gardens Kenton did not relinquish his hold, nor did Joanne attempt to move from it as they followed the comtesse and Dr. Ames into the Rotunda.

Dancing had already begun and Joanne watched with a heavy heart the graceful movements of the dancers which were accentuated by the brilliant array of coloured hoods and gowns. The lights were brighter, the people gayer, everything intensified because of Kenton's presence beside her.

Insistent upon dancing, the comtesse drew Ames away.

"Would you care to dance?" Kenton asked Joanne stiffly.

"Only if you wish, my lord," she answered with equal reserve.

What does she think, feel? he questioned silently as he gazed at her, his longing clear to all but Joanne. *Dare I take the chance? Why do you hesitate?* His heart beat strongly. *She is no longer the girl-child who thought of you as a father.*

A careless reveler stumbled into Kenton, pushing him against Joanne. Reaching out to regain his balance, he found her in his arms. Reason forced him to drop his hold. If only we could be alone, he cursed to himself, looking past Joanne into the gay crowd of people surrounding them.

"Let us dance, my lord," Joanne breathed, the comtesse forgotten as hope surged. Had she read his gaze aright?

Their eyes met—held. Trancelike, they joined the dancers. Heartbeat answered heartbeat as they moved through the motions of the dance, conscious only of each other. The magic ended as Joanne was claimed for the next dance when the music stopped. A steady stream of partners, all of whom teased her to guess who they were, kept Jason frustratingly far away. At last she pled fatigue and sought the comtesse's petite form among those standing at the side. She caught sight of her and made to join her. A hand grabbed her arm and Joanne swung about angrily to face a giggling, masked face.

"Do you not know me?" questioned Lady Sarah. "I

am so glad you wore the yellow gown. I never would have found you otherwise. Isn't this thrilling?" she rattled on. "Oh, I almost forgot. Let me pin these on your domino." She raised a posy of yellow roses.

"Why are you doing this?" Joanne asked. "Where did you get them?"

"You have a secret beau," Sarah laughed conspiratorially. "No, I won't tell you who it is, but he wished to be able to tell you from the others for a certainty. I promise you will know who it is before the eve is o'er," she said with a sly smile.

Joanne fingered the delicate flowers lying beautifully amid baby's breath. "It is only your cousin, Humbolt," she sighed, evoking a fresh stream of giggles from Sarah.

"As you will," the girl said with a wink. "I think your beau will offer for you." Claimed for a dance, she was gone before Joanne could question her further.

"Why what lovely flowers," the comtesse exclaimed when Joanne joined her. "But where did they come from?"

"Lady Sarah pinned them to me—some nonsense about a secret beau," Joanne answered with casual annoyance. "Most likely they are from Humbolt," she said, dismissing the subject. "Is Benjamin or Lord Jason near? I must admit to a terrible thirst and this heat," she fanned herself, "is quite stifling. Is there always such a crush?"

"But why ask me?" her aunt laughed. "Do you not believe I have kept to my home before we met? Oh, I tease you," she said lightly as she saw Joanne's puzzled reaction. "There is Dr. Ames, and Lord Kenton is with him. Let us claim them. Something cool to drink and a walk in the evening air would be most welcome."

"But surely we should not go into the gardens?" Joanne questioned, thinking of her aunt's reprimands.

"A group is always respectable," the comtesse tossed back and took Joanne's hand. Quickly they reached the men's sides.

The gentlemen about Kenton and Ames welcomed them cordially. The comtesse, recognizing some, teased them lightly. During the interplay Joanne was asked to dance. She refused, but the man was insistent. Not wishing to be the cause of an embarrassing scene, she finally acquiesced.

"Do the flowers please you, my lady?" the man asked as he led Joanne toward the assembling dancers.

"Lord Wiltham?" she questioned, cocking her head. In surprise she asked, "Was it you who sent them?"

"A token of my affection—which I hope you return," he said smoothly. "It is but the first of many testimonials of my love."

"Love, my lord?" Joanne asked, startled. "But I have never encour . . ." Her words trailed off as remembrances of her behaviour flooded back. "Oh, my lord . . ."

"Now is not the time to speak—later, my love. Let us watch our steps; we would not wish anyone to guess our secret."

Blanching, Joanne swallowed. Her movements were mechanical as she wrestled with the problem. The dance ended all too quickly. Ames's appearance at her side rescued her from an immediate confrontation. Wiltham bowed, kissing her hand. "Till later," he murmured.

"Are you feeling ill?" Benjamin asked, noting her sudden lack of colour.

"I . . . I am fine," she managed. "Where is the comtesse?"

"With Kenton—we go to join them now."

"Mayhap, they would rather remain alone," Joanne ventured weakly, remembering her resolve.

"What would cause you to say that?" scoffed Benjamin.

"They are of an age," she began as they walked from the Rotunda. The breeze brushed by with a cooling caress. "Oh, the air is delightful."

"Here, over here," the comtesse's voice chimed.

The two glanced about. "There." Ames proceeded toward the two.

Kenton handed Ames a glass of wine and the comtesse gave Joanne a half-melted ice. Freed of the second glass, the comtesse took Ames's arm. "Come, Benjamin, I need a walk in this invigorating air. Joanne, my lord, will you follow?" she asked over her shoulder as they started out.

"We had best go with them," Kenton said, seeing Joanne's hesitation. "They could become lost," he attempted to joke as he held out his arm. Mentally sighing, Joanne put her hand on it and matched his steps.

A leisurely pace was set by the comtesse as she led them down shadowy paths and past fountains, pools reflecting silver ripples in the bright moonlight.

On they walked, the first pair gradually putting greater distance between them. The sounds of the revelers slowly diminished and the soothing night air slowly relaxed the two stiff figures of the latter pair.

"It is beautiful here," Joanne murmured.

"No more lovely than you," Kenton said, before thinking could forestall the words.

Joanne stopped and turned toward him. "What, my lord?" she breathed.

Her wide eyes and wondering, hopeful expression drew Kenton nearer. The shackles he had put on his desire were cast aside as Joanne stepped toward him. Emotion ruled as his arms closed about her and their lips met. Joy rushed through her as Jason's arms tightened about her, as his lips gently moved across her own. A flame leaped within as she responded to his growing urgency.

Ahead, the two figures reappeared in the moonlight. The smaller poked the taller in the ribs. Both smiled broadly at the embracing couple before disappearing again.

Forcing himself to draw back, Kenton gazed in wonder at Joanne. Neither spoke, the wonder of their love too great. They kissed again—a slow lingering kiss.

"I love you," Joanne breathed softly.

Kenton tightened his arms about her. Drunken laughter intruded. He stiffened. "We must be going; we must not be seen alone here," came from him regretfully.

"But why?" Joanne questioned, an amused softness in her voice.

He stole a quick kiss and, taking her arm, began to retrace their steps. "This is most improper," he said and both shared laughter at the thought.

All too quickly they were amid others. Glancing

at Kenton, Joanne wondered if she dreamed the moment, until he turned his gaze to hers and she saw the shadows of desire. No, it was true, she thought happily. The glow of her love shone brightly.

Looking at her Kenton's fears were erased, all his hopes answered. Impatience was mastered with the surety of the future. His nonchalant manner caused the eyebrows that had been raised at their returning alone to sink in disappointment. However, one in particular was angered at seeing the two together.

Wiltham toyed with the corner of his lapel. The time was near—the stage set. But he would see this matter taken care of first. He cared not for the way Joanne looked at Kenton nor the man's possessive smile. Claiming her for a country set, Wiltham did not speak until the intricate steps ended. "Was that your friend, Kenton?" he asked casually.

"Why, yes," Joanne returned, not realizing how much her tender tone revealed.

"I wish I had his success," Wiltham responded with some bitterness.

"Why, what do you mean, Lord Wiltham?" she asked, her eyes seeking Jason.

"His success with the ladies is so unbelievable," he began, "but pardon me, I should never have spoken of it."

"Surely you jest?" Joanne asked sharply.

"What is said and what I have seen is not for your ears, my lady," Wiltham answered protectively.

The cold hand of fear gripped Joanne. "But he is a true gentleman," she insisted.

"As you say," he answered with just enough haste

to win his point. The seed of doubt was sown. "There are many who say he specializes in green girls but I do not believe it," Wiltham added for good measure. Motioning toward the boxes, he asked, "Would you care to sit awhile?"

"Yes, but first I must find the comtesse," Joanne answered distractedly, her mind reeling beneath Wiltham's implications.

"You will find she is busy," Wiltham tossed back offhandedly. "Here is my box. Rest for a few moments while I search for her. Or would your friend, Lady Sarah, do as well?"

"Yes, that would be most kind of you, Lord Wiltham," she replied, taking a seat.

"I will return shortly."

She nodded, thinking vaguely that perhaps she had misjudged him. Fanning herself lightly, she looked about, searching for the familiar figure with the rust jacket and black domino. It should not be difficult to pick him out, she thought; I have seen no other of that colour. What Lord Wiltham said is preposterous, she tried to reassure herself. If Jason were what the man suggested, would he not have attempted to seduce me at Kentoncombe? But, what reason did Wiltham have to lie? He was even sorry the subject had been broached. There was no reason not to believe him except for her faith in Kenton. Was she wise to trust Jason? Was there anyone she could truly rely upon?

A rust-coloured arm raised in salute caught her eye. But this man had his other arm about a . . . a wanton. Her hand raised to her breast as she saw him kissing her. With her stomach doing a sickening flop, she looked away. It could not be Jason—but she had to know. Looking back, she studied the man. He was of Kenton's height—even the hair colour was the same. Let it not be, she cried softly. Her eyes frantically swept the crowd, seeking the sight of another rust-coloured jacket, but none was to be seen.

Wiltham returned and followed her stricken gaze. A wicked smile appeared, then was disguised into concern. "You are quite pale, my lady. I did not find the comtesse, but I learned Lady Sarah is just outside on the steps. Let us join her. The air will revive you." He took her arm and she rose. "Pay no attention to Kenton," he said when she moved no further. "They say he always behaves thusly—taking his pleasure from any willing woman."

Throwing a beseeching look at Wiltham, she asked, "You saw his face? It is Kenton?"

He nodded confidently. "I passed quite near—but this distresses you. Let us join Lady Sarah."

Joanne did not resist the touch of his hand urging her forward.

"But I thought you said Lady Sarah was just on the steps," Joanne questioned suddenly, realizing Wiltham had led her quite a distance from the Rotunda and that the light was growing much dimmer.

"I believe she is just ahead—see her there. We shall just have a few steps to go. If it is not she, we will return to the Rotunda and look for Comtesse de Clarté," he assured her.

The figure he had pointed to faded as they neared.

"We must turn back," Joanne said, fear leaping to the fore of her disheveled emotions.

"We must go—but not back to the Rotunda," Wiltham said with bald confidence.

"What do you mean?" Joanne demanded. Suddenly realization dawned. "You knew Lady Sarah was not here. How dare you?" Anger sparked her words. "I will go nowhere with you." Turning from him, she found her arm fastly held.

"These gentlemen are here to help us depart—quite unnoticed, I assure you," Wiltham bragged.

Four men had appeared from the shadows. Panicking, Joanne opened her mouth to scream and found a hand close upon it cruelly. She clawed at it with her free hand. Cursing, the man grabbed her arm and wrenched it behind her back.

"Now, my haughty beauty," Wiltham sneered as he watched her futile struggle, "we will be off to call upon your father."

Kicking out violently, Joanne fought to twist free of their hold. *Jason! Jason!* her mind screamed. The anger that had strengthened her slowly dissolved—her efforts gained only tightened grips, more painful restraints. *Oh, Lord,* she prayed, *let Jason rescue me.*

They forced a gag into her mouth; her hands were bound. She was roughly pulled along the path and pushed hurriedly into a waiting coach.

Wiltham settled in beside her, his hand cupping her chin. "How unfortunate you are not willing in this. It could be so enjoyable for us both." His hand dropped to her breast.

Shuddering, Joanne flung herself away from his touch.

With a derisive laugh Wiltham leaned back in his corner of the coach.

Terror wriggled into Joanne's mind as remembrances of the drunken encounter at Furness House flooded back. Then she had escaped. Would she now?

Chapter Twenty-two

Concern gnawed at the comtesse. Kenton should have returned Joanne to her side by now. Men are unpredictable when in love, she thought, but . . . "Ah, Dr. Ames. Have you seen Lord Jason or Lady Joanne?"

"I believe I saw them come in some time ago. Ah, here is Jason now.

"Good eve, once again, my lord," Ames greeted him, striving to remain in control of his smile.

"Is Joanne not with you?" Kenton asked, glancing at those standing nearby.

"We thought she was with you," the comtesse returned.

"But I have not seen her for over an hour."

"Perhaps she is with Lady Sarah," Ames offered.

"Which is she?" Kenton asked, looking at the gossiping women. "How can you tell one from another?"

"It is quite easy, my lord," the comtesse said archly. "I see Sarah now." She hurried up to the slightly larger figure. "Lady Sarah, may I speak with you?"

"Of course, Comtesse. Is this not the grandest

masque? I think it is very bad-mannered of Humbolt to insist we leave. He is ill-tempered as a baited bear this eve."

"But why?"

"Oh, he has danced only once with Lady Joanne and has not been able even to speak with her but for a few seconds. It would not surprise me," Sarah leaned forward and lowered her voice, "if he meant to offer for Joanne. It would have been nice to have had her for a cousin," she ended reflectively.

"But why are you certain she would not agree to the match?" the comtesse asked, instinct causing her to probe.

"Because, well, Lord Wiltham said . . ." She stopped guiltily.

"Then the flowers you pinned to Joanne's domino were from Wiltham." The comtesse took Lady Sarah's hand. "Come with me," she ordered. "We go outdoors," she clipped to Kenton and Ames as she brushed past.

The two followed, their curiosity raised at this turn. Outside the Rotunda, the comtesse led Lady Sarah to a bench away from most of the crowd and directed her to sit.

"Now you will tell me about this business with Lord Wiltham," she commanded.

Sarah looked nervously from the petite figure with hands on her hips to Kenton, then down to her folded hands. "But I promised . . ."

"There is no need to fear breaking a promise. Wiltham had you pin the flowers on Joanne's domino so he would be certain it was she—*n'est-ce pas?*"

A nod affirmed it. "But there was nothing wrong in doing that," Sarah defended her action.

"No one has said you have done wrong," Kenton said assuringly. "Simply tell us what you know."

"Well . . ." she looked at the three searchingly. "I suppose it is all right. Lord Wiltham promised . . . he said he would do me a favour . . . if I could convince Joanne to come to the masque. Then tonight he gave me the flowers. I thought it odd he wished me to do it, especially when he said they were to be married."

"Married!" Jason snapped.

Frightened by Kenton's tone, Lady Sarah broke into tears. "I meant no harm, truly I did not," she cried.

"We believe you, child," the comtesse consoled her. "Benjamin, fetch Lord Humbolt. Tell him his cousin is not feeling well and must be taken home."

Ames hurried to do as bid. Sitting beside Sarah, Kenton asked gently, "Did Wiltham say anything else? Did Joanne give any indication she was agreeable or even knowledgeable of his intentions? Think carefully."

"I don't recall anything else Lord Wiltham said," Sarah sobbed, "and Joanne didn't speak of marrying anyone." Taking the kerchief the comtesse offered, she blew her nose forcefully. Subsiding into sniffles, she added, "Why, Joanne did not act as if she cared for Humbolt to ask for her hand—so it had to be Wiltham she cares for. I thought I was helping her."

"Humbolt plans to ask for her hand . . ." began Kenton.

"That is of no matter now," the comtesse cut him off. "If she is with Wiltham, there is every reason to fear for her."

"Comtesse de Clarté, Lord Kenton," Humbolt greeted them. "Dr. Ames says my cousin is ill. Sarah, what is wrong?"

"She has only the headache—too much excitement," the comtesse told him lightly. "Just take her home and she will be fine."

"But I wish to speak with Lady Joanne," Humbolt objected.

"It seems many have the same desire this eve," she twittered with false airiness. "She is dancing now. I will tell her you shall call upon us on the morrow," he was assured. After a slight hesitation Humbolt bowed. "Thank you, my lady. Come, Sarah." He held out his hand to help her rise.

"Everything will be all right, won't it?" Sarah asked the comtesse.

"Yes, child, never fear. We shall be seeing you soon. Good eve."

When the two were beyond hearing range, Kenton exploded. "What has been happening? What is this about Joanne and Wiltham?"

"Please calm yourself, Lord Jason. Do you wish everyone to hear? First, I do not believe she favours him. I have learned a little about the man and it all points to a scheme from Furness," the comtesse explained impatiently.

"A scheme? What do you know?"

"Lord Perton told me that until two months ago Lord Wiltham owed money to every merchant in London. There were rumours his estates were to be confiscated for payment. Then suddenly all debts were cleared and ever since Wiltham has been paying for everything at the time of purchase. This is odd enough, but Lord Perton also said that until this time Wiltham was in Furness's pocket."

"You believe Furness has set Wiltham to woo Joanne?" Ames asked. "Why would he?"

"It makes sense," Kenton threw in, thinking of Furness and what he knew of the relationship between father and daughter.

"I am glad you agree," the comtesse said, arching an eyebrow and walking swiftly toward the exits.

"But where are you going?" Ames called out.

"You cannot believe Joanne would agree to marrying him without telling me," flared the comtesse. She snapped her fingers in Kenton's face. "That is how much you care for her to let her be tied to a dog selected by her father. I for one do not believe she left willingly. And I intend doing something about it. Benjamin," she said expectantly.

"She may be right," Ames said, stepping to her side.

"And what would you have us do?" Kenton asked, fear, anger, and confusion mingling. His heart told him Joanne loved him. His ears had heard her words but his eyes had also seen her flirt outrageously with Wiltham and Humbolt. Had she spoken of love to them also?

"We should go to Furness's lodgings at once," the comtesse insisted. "He will know the direction Wiltham has taken. Then we pursue them."

"I will come, but even if Furness allows us entry, I doubt we will learn anything from him." Kenton looked so woebegone, her heart yearned to comfort him. "Have you not thought we both have been played for fools?" his doubts prompted him to say.

"No," she flashed and started once again for the exits, glancing back only to see that Ames and Kenton followed.

"Daughter, how pleasant to see you," Furness greeted Joanne as the two men who had carried her put her in the chair and departed. Confronted with her father, unable to escape him, her old hate and fears surged viciously back. She struggled to be free of the rope binding her hands behind her back.

"I fear you do not have a very biddable bride, my lord," he said with a stark laugh to Wiltham. "But then she was never a biddable daughter." He downed the half glass of port in his hand and refilled it.

"A few lessons on the proper treatment of a husband is all she requires," Wiltham tossed back with lighter accents than his quavering spirit felt.

"Let us drink to your success." Furness held forth a goblet of wine which the other took eagerly and emptied in a single draught. With a mocking smile, Furness refilled it and raised his own in salute.

The second glass downed, Wiltham began, "The papers, my lord. You said we would sign the papers when . . ."

"They are ready—over there." He motioned to a sideboard. "Look them over if you will—they require only your signature. My man has witnessed my signature already," he said, refilling his drink as he stared at his daughter. Her hair was dark where Joanna's had been light. But the eyes—they reminded him of . . . He drank slowly.

Eagerly Wiltham had picked up the documents and read them. "Most agreeable, my lord, most generous," he commented after several minutes. "Where do I sign?"

"If you had read closely, you would have seen that the contract is with my daughter's husband." He forced his eyes from Joanne. "Do you have the special license?"

Wiltham dug inside his coat and pulled forth the rolled parchment.

"Good. When the ceremony is done, you may sign," Furness told him.

Joanne listened with disbelief. Her father was willing to pay this man? What have I ever done? Why this when all I ever wanted was love?

"Where is the cleric then—why do we waste time?" Wiltham demanded anxiously.

"See what an impatient bridegroom you have," Furness said, turning to Joanne. He walked to her side, feeling a sudden impulse to touch her, and startled himself as his hand moved slowly toward her. She wrenched away. I was right, his ugly pride asserted itself, to have loathed her existence. A twinge of guilt hit Furness but he killed it with thoughts of his daughter's prideful arrogance. I was right, he assured himself. He forced himself to speak calmly. "Why, my dear, I was merely going to undo this contrivance."

Joanne forced herself to bear her father's touch as he untied the rough chafing cloth about her mouth.

Free of it, she found her throat too parched to allow speech and she accepted the goblet he held to her lips. The burning port hit her stomach with wrenching swiftness. She gasped.

"Not accustomed to drink," Furness laughed maliciously. "I believe that will change." His mood shifted and he ordered, "Untie her."

"Is that wise, my lord?" quaked the prospective bridegroom.

"Where will she go—what harm can she do?" Furness questioned. "You think to run to the comtesse?" he asked Joanne, "or perhaps . . . to Kenton?" Years of experience had taught him Joanne's vulnerabilities. He had keenly honed his skill in deflating her—of wrenching any security from her. At mention of Kenton's name he saw the hope spring to her eyes and a devil of old bade him quash it.

"Think again. What will the reaction be when the tale of your sojourn at Kentoncombe is told abroad, when everyone learns your dear comtesse participated also? What of her reputation then?"

"Nothing happened there," Joanne retorted, rising to defend those he threatened.

"Would you have me believe that? I am no fool. You have become," he waved a hand and leered, "attractive. Kenton, I have learned, is a widower of many years. He must have delighted in you, my dear." His tone slurred the love Joanne held dear. "And the comtesse's charms—I envy the man."

Fury spurred Joanne and she struck at her father.

He dropped his glass and caught her hand. "Ah, you did not enjoy sharing him?"

"You foul beast," she began.

Furness threw her roughly into the chair and slapped her face, throwing her back sharply. His hands locked onto the chair's arms. He pushed his face to within inches of hers. "Listen well, my dear," he snarled. "I can ruin the comtesse, Kenton, and you, if that is your wish. Simply leave here and it is done."

Her body recoiling from his blow, her mind reeling from his words, Joanne saw the drunken glare in her father's eyes. *He will do anything to satisfy what consumes him,* she thought. A new fear arose—not for herself but for Jason.

The fury evoked by her defiance slowly died. Furness loosened his hold and straightened. Regaining control, he casually adjusted his stock. Claiming a new glass, he filled it and faced her again. "But if you have some feeling . . . some affection," his tone made the word a curse, "for them, think again. Marry Wiltham and they will be spared. Think on it, but quickly. I want the answer . . . now."

Conflicting thoughts vied with each other as Joanne tried to reason. Too much had occurred too quickly. There had to be some way to protect the comtesse, to shield Jason from her father's vilification and yet to save herself. Time . . . I must have time to think.

"What is your answer?" Furness demanded. He waited only a moment. "Throw her into the street, Wiltham," he ordered, turning away.

"But, my lord . . ." the younger man objected, seeing his fortune slipping away.

"Turn her out," he leered at Joanne. "We shall see how welcome the comtesse is in society when I am finished. Why I shall be forced to demand satisfaction from Lord Kenton for ruining my daughter."

"No," breathed Joanne. His final words made her decision for her. Her love for Jason gave her strength; she would not save herself and lose all by losing him. All her life her father's threats had been carried out. In this time when duels were commonplace, their legality avidly defended, there was no doubt he would do as he said. Intensifying her resolve was the knowledge that Furness was an excellent shot. Since her arrival in London she had heard of at least five men he had killed in such meetings. She would not let him add Kenton to the list.

"What did you say?" Furness asked softly, triumph in his eyes.

"I will . . . will marry your . . . pawn," she choked out.

Furness pulled the bell cord hanging near the door. A liveried footman entered. "Bring the minister," his master ordered.

"Yes, my lord," he answered, withdrawing as quickly as he had come.

"May I write the comtesse?" Joanne asked, seeking any way to delay.

"Of course, as soon as the ceremony is ended," her father answered cordially. "Ah, Reverend Monroe," he greeted the bent, gray-haired figure that stumbled into the room.

Joanne stared at the old man—his hands a constant tremble, his head atwitch. The smell of spirits was strongly about him.

"This is my daughter, Lady Joanne," she heard her father say, "and Lord Wiltham." His hand forced her to stand beside him. "Let us begin."

The palsied reverend opened a prayer book so new the pages cracked as they were turned. "C-could ye c-come c-closer," he stuttered.

Is there no escape, Joanne thought frantically. *Jason, will you not save me?*

"Do ye ta-take . . . th-this mannnn," the cleric's voice stumbled on.

For a wild moment Joanne thought again to flee, but the bite of her father's hand bespoke his threats.

". . . to . . . be yer law . . . lawful . . . wed . . . ded sp-spouse."

Unable to escape—unable to flee without condemning those she loved, Joanne turned her thoughts to a safe, hidden chamber of her mind. She retreated from reality as she had retreated as a child from the verbal onslaughts of her father. In moments she knew the answer to the cleric's stuttered vows would be demanded. She gathered strength to follow her resolve.

"Joanne," her father's voice penetrated. "Answer."

She looked to him in a last desperate plea.

"Answer."

Faint shouts and curses, the sounds of scuffling in the corridor jerked Furness's head toward the door. "Say it," he rasped, "say it."

"I . . . I . . . I do," Joanne's spirit surrendered.

Chapter Twenty-three

The door burst open behind Furness. Jason Kenton shrugged off a footman trying to stop him and grabbed at a second.

"Enough," Furness called out, ending the scuffle.

Dr. Ames struggled up from the floor in the corridor as the man atop him stood. Stepping over a prone figure, the comtesse joined the two.

"Lord Kenton, my lady," Furness bowed. "You have arrived in time to witness the last of the marriage vows. Joanne has already spoken hers. Continue," he told the cleric sharply.

"D-do ye . . ."

"Wait." Kenton's voice rang in the room. His eyes had not left Joanne's back.

"Joanne cannot be willing in this," the comtesse protested.

"Tell them," Furness demanded confidently.

The joy that had sprung to life in Joanne at the sound of Jason's voice ebbed away. He had come to save her but if she allowed him to rescue her, she would condemn him.

"Did you consent to this marriage?" Jason asked hollowly.

The comtesse flew to Joanne's side, brushed Furness's hand from her arm. "Tell him you did not, *ma chère*, tell him."

"But I have agreed," Joanne forced herself to say, still refusing to turn and look at them.

Kenton came to her side and slowly turned her to him. "Do you love him?" he asked, his hand reaching out to take hers.

She nodded, her eyes begging forgiveness of the lie.

Bitter anger boiled up within Kenton. "This is your doing," he clipped, turning to Furness.

"She has told you of her agreement—there is nothing you can do, my lord," sneered the harsh-faced figure. "Did you not have enough satisfaction from sampling her charms while she stayed with you?"

Kenton's fist snapped out and Furness dropped to the floor.

The comtesse applauded and Wiltham cringed— pulling Joanne before him like a shield. She herself stood in uncomprehending disbelief.

"It is more than his doing," Benjamin said. He had entered quietly and seeing the papers, leafed through them. These he now handed to Kenton saying, "Read the terms herein."

A groan escaped from Furness as he struggled to sit. One of the liveried servants standing in the doorway rushed to help him rise. "Get out," Furness snarled, "get out and shut that door." The servant tripped in his hurry to leave, staggered through the door, and slammed it shut behind him.

Rising slowly, Furness eyed Kenton, hatred in his

every line. "I demand satisfaction." Venom dripped from the words.

"You shall have it," Kenton answered, glancing up from the documents he was reading, "but this matter will be taken care of first." He turned to Joanne. "You have agreed to this marriage but I believe it was not done willingly. I cannot stand by and let your life be ruined."

"You cannot prevent this," roared Furness.

"These documents say I can," Kenton said with deadly calm. "You know what the result would be if I had them published."

Fury choked Furness. He lunged for the papers.

"I wouldn't do that, my lord," Ames said, stepping ahead of Kenton. "One of your men had no further use for this," he added, pointing a flintlock pistol at Furness's chest.

Impotent rage gripped the man; he did not move.

Ignoring him, Kenton returned his attention to Joanne. "These papers secure all that is not entailed, and provide a generous allowance during the earl's life—they need only be signed by your husband. If it is Humbolt you want, he will have you. You need not go to him dowerless." He handed the papers to the comtesse. "Give these to a trusted solicitor—he will know what to do. Now, take Joanne—wed her to Humbolt with all haste. Go now."

Trembling under Kenton's gaze, Wiltham stepped away from Joanne. The comtesse put her arm about Joanne's waist and tugged, but the young woman did not move. Her battered spirit trembled. Why did he speak of Humbolt? What could she say?

"Go," snapped Kenton angrily, "you will thank me one day for doing this."

Defeated by his look, tone, and words, she slumped, but caught herself and the comtesse hurried her from the room.

When the women were gone, Kenton spoke to Furness. "The choice of weapons is yours."

"Pistols," spat the other.

"Hyde Park at first light?"

Furness nodded.

"My second will be Dr. Ames."

"Wiltham will have to do for mine," Furness returned, looking with disgust at the frightened figure who neither moved nor ventured to speak.

"Ames will settle the details with him." Bowing formally, Kenton straightened, turned, and strode from the room.

"I take it there is no chance for settling this peacefully?" Ames asked Furness, fulfilling that part of his duty.

"Speak to Wiltham, Doctor. I shall see Kenton dead at first light."

"We are home, come," the comtesse said coaxingly. Joanne looked past her to confirm the fact; she had not thought to see these doors again.

The footman handed the women down the coach's steps. The small French butler stood beside the open door.

"We are happy to see you returned, *madame,*" he greeted the women.

"Dr. Ames and Lord Kenton may come soon . . . or

at early light. When they do they are to be shown into the morning room immediately," she ordered.

"*Oui, madame,*" he answered. His mistress's looks and tone suggested concern, urgency. Throwing open the doors to the morning room, he proceeded to light the candles and lamps. The comtesse gave him their dominos as she entered.

"Do you wish something brought, *madame*?"

"*Oui,* brandy, please," she answered without looking, hovering beside Joanne.

Certainement. A duel came to the butler's mind as he recalled her words—at early light. He bowed and went for the brandy.

The morning room was set so that the full wall of windows faced east. Catching the full force of the rising sun, it was a cheerful place in which to take the morning's repast. Even later in the day it was a favourite haunt of the women, its yellow-sprigged paper encouraging lightness and gaiety. The Louis Quatorze furniture, brought from France, was light and airy. The comtesse's unique use of decorative plants instead of massive family portraits or the clutter of small trivia set an attractive tone.

Joanne saw none of this as she stood before the windows—now a wall of black which only threw her reflection accusingly back at her.

"*Ma chère,* drink this. You are shivering."

Obedient because it was easiest, Joanne took the small glass and drained it. The smooth brandy spread a burst of warmth through her. "Will it be today?" she asked.

The comtesse's first thought was to feign ignorance

but her niece's look stayed that. These were the first words Joanne had spoken since leaving Furness's quarters; there was to be no pretense.

"It is probable that it will be this morn—at sunrise. That is the preferred time for such happenings," she answered softly.

"I could have tried to dissuade him," Joanne said despairingly.

"*Non,* it would have been *impossible.* Men regard their honour highly; none may interfere where it is concerned. Someday the duel will be prohibited, but for now," the comtesse sighed, "we can do little but wait. Let us sit—or perhaps you wish to retire, to undress?"

"No . . . no." Joanne moved about randomly, the vacant look of her eyes unchanging. "How did you know where to find me?" she asked, sitting in a chair that faced the windows.

"We were going to Furness to ask Wiltham's direction—Lady Sarah told us he had said the two of you were to be wed," the comtesse added in explanation. "When I stepped out of the coach before his doors, I saw the posy Lady Sarah had pinned to your domino —we knew then you were inside. Kenton fought like a madman when they did not want to let us enter. Benjamin did no less," she added conscientiously. "Thank God we were in time."

"Would that you had never come."

"But why say that?" The comtesse moved to stand before her.

"He will kill Jason—even if he fails in that, all of you will be ruined," Joanne answered dully.

"It is true he may kill Lord Jason. Dueling is inviting death." She grabbed Joanne's hand as the other winced at the words. "But it is just as likely Lord Jason will kill Furness."

Something in Joanne's eyes flickered. The awful emptiness began to yield to a faint hope.

Scenes of life at Kentoncombe filled Joanne: Jason at work in the fields, with the farm stock, with his men. *He is a good man, a kind man,* she thought, *and I love him. Then think,* her subconscious prodded her on. *Think how he taught you to reason—to control your temper, your fears. He gave you strength by having confidence in you. Use it now.* She shook her head. The danger of losing him was too great. Life without him would be too empty. Suddenly a gleam, a small glimpse of understanding at what her father had felt on losing her mother pierced her. His sorrow had twisted him, had cost them both dearly. Now sorrow added to her fear of losing Jason. She surrendered to the tears that could no longer be held back.

The utter desolation of her niece wrenched the comtesse's heart. She put her arms about Joanne's shoulders and held her tightly till the sobs eased.

"How did Wiltham take you from Ranelagh?" she asked, trying to distract Joanne as she struggled to regain her composure.

"I told him I must find you. He had said something about Jason that upset me and insisted I go to Sarah, that she was just on the steps outside the Rotunda. I was so perturbed that before I realized it we were on the garden paths with Sarah nowhere to be seen.

"He had four men waiting," Joanne continued disgustedly. "After they bound my hands and gagged me, they took me to my father." Her face contorted as she strove not to let the tears break loose once again. "If only it were I that could die—to bring so much harm to the only two who have ever shown me kindness is unbearable."

"What is this to talk of ruin?"

"My father said he would . . . he would tell horrible tales a-about my stay at Kentoncombe . . . and about you also."

"Is that all," the comtesse laughed with relief. "After this night he will not dare anything."

"Are those papers so condemning?"

"Enough for the purpose. Do not worry," the comtesse paused, studying Joanne. "I ask you to speak openly now. What occurred between you and Lord Jason this eve?"

A blush swept to Joanne's face; then confusion caused it to fade. "I am . . . uncertain. Uncertain at least of the meaning," she said with eyes downcast.

"Tell me and then we shall see what meaning there can be."

"We were walking and I commented on something, I don't even recall what, but Jason said I was . . . lovely." She savoured the recollection. "It was as if suddenly we were all alone, that no one existed but us."

"Ah, *oui*, I remember that feeling," the comtesse sighed.

"Jason looked at me so and then we . . . kissed." The sweet sensation, the thrill of his lips over hers, flashed through Joanne.

"And?" prompted her aunt.

"And then someone laughed and Jason said it would

not do to be found alone and he hurried me back to the Rotunda," Joanne grimaced. "Lord Wiltham claimed me for a dance the moment we entered. I had no chance to speak with Jason and he said nothing."

"But you thought the kiss was a promise?"

"Well, yes. But then Lord Wiltham told me how Jason's reputation for chasing light skirts was well known . . . and . . . I saw him kissing a . . . a wanton." Her last words were barely audible.

"You *saw* Jason Kenton actually kissing a courtesan?" the comtesse asked in disbelief.

"I did not see his face, but his was the only rust-coloured coat I saw all eve. Wiltham said he did see his face and it was Jason."

"Did you ask how he knew for a certainty who it was with everyone being masked? Don't fret about it," she hurried on. "He was clever for the moment and circumstances aided him. It matters not."

"But it does—for just as I believed that it was he, Jason believes . . . oh, I don't know what. But he does not love me—how could he and tell me to wed Humbolt?" She looked completely confused and dismayed.

"Goosefeathers!" The comtesse laughed at Joanne's expression. "Oh, your face says more than many words I could have chosen," she noted and was rewarded with a wan smile.

"Men are never more muddle-headed than when they fear for someone they love, and Lord Jason had had a frightful start over you.

"When this is past and he has had time to think the matter through clearly he will see his error, you shall see." She glanced toward the windows. "Dawn will come soon. Let us pray God will be good to the just."

Yes, thought Joanne, *be just.* Jason's features played before her eyes. *He taught me so much,* she marveled. *So much I never realized.*

Far away in the sky a shooting star flared, lighting the windowpane, and then died. *Jason is like that star,* Joanne thought. *He lit my life, bringing me from darkness.*

An inner calm came over her. "I will not betray your teaching, my love," she whispered, her hand reaching out to touch the pane where the star had shone. *God forbid you be lost to me, but if you are, you have taught me how to go on. You will be with me always.*

The coach's team nickered and stamped restlessly in the damp morning air of Hyde Park. Inside, a single candle burned low. Kenton reached inside his coat and drew out a sealed letter which he handed to Ames. "Take this to the comtesse—no matter what the results of this be." A hand tiredly waved aside Ames's objection. "It merely tells her how to use the documents we gave her. When Joanne is wed, they must be signed and secured from Furness."

"Did you ever think that Joanne might not wish to marry Humbolt?" Ames retorted, sadness leavening his anger. "Will you have no words for her?"

"She is lucky anyone will wed her," came the curt reply, caused by doubts and the strain of events upon him.

"I certainly was wrong then—about you both," Ames spoke freely at last. "Fool that I am, I thought you loved her, but you have judged her without a word on her part."

"Be done—they come."

The jingle of harness and dull thuds of hooves affirmed Kenton's words. Ames followed him from the coach bearing a box of matched dueling pistols.

Furness eyed Kenton speculatively. A sense of shame came over him at the other's unwavering gaze but was pushed aside. "I have killed many men . . ." he began.

"That matters not to me," clipped Lord Jason. "I damn you for trying to destroy your daughter."

"My daughter." The curse had lost its flavour. All night he had battled dreams of his wife, Joanna, poised shielding Joanne. As sobriety returned he began to see that his hatred had been a self-pitying, all-consuming passion to punish his daughter for the loss of his wife. His mind reeled under the condemning recollection. Staggered, he pushed his thoughts aside and pulled the bottle of port nearer to comfort him as it had always done in the past. Too many years—too much twisted pride—was involved for him to turn too quickly in his ways. Drinking deeply, repeatedly, his guilt was drowned, his rationalizations bolstered. "Do you really think she is worth dying for?" he asked Kenton.

"Would you have believed your wife was?" Kenton answered and turned to Ames, who helped him remove his coat.

Wiltham assisted Furness. There was to be no turning back. The dueling pistol cases were opened for each to make their choice. The selection made, Kenton and Furness stood back to back.

"I shall count fourteen paces," Wiltham said shakily. His voice quavered and he began, "One . . . two . . ."

Fourteen was called; the two men turned and faced each other. A shot rang into the quiet morning; a second sounded on the first's echo. One figure lay fallen upon the grass.

"You are not hit?" Ames exclaimed running up to Kenton.

"I felt it pass," he answered coldly. "See to Furness," Kenton ordered, taking his coat. He returned to the coach and put the dueling pistol in its case, snapping it shut angrily. What had been achieved? Pulling on his coat, he walked to where Ames was kneeling over Furness. "Is it serious?"

"The ball passed through his body, I believe. If it missed his lungs or any other vital organ, he may live," Ames answered as he worked to stem the flow of blood.

Furness opened his eyes. "Damn you," he cursed. "It misfired."

"I did not wish for your life," Kenton told him. "This ends it."

"I have had my revenge," Furness gasped. He attempted to laugh but it came out a groan. "You are wedding her to Humbolt but it is you she . . . loves."

"She could have loved you," Kenton told him. "You could have had so much more. Was it worth it?" He eyed the man pityingly.

"What need did I have for love with my Joanna dead?" he rasped, his breath becoming laboured.

"When did you ever have more need of it? Think

on it. You loved the mother—the daughter is equally deserving.

"See that he lives," Kenton told Ames and turned away.

"I will come to the comtesse's when I have finished," he called after Kenton.

"Give her the letter then."

"But surely you go there now—they will be expecting it."

Kenton shook his head. "I don't know where I shall go. Away. Away from London . . . but not to Kentoncombe." He strode away before Ames could speak.

The fool, Ames said to himself as he watched the coach wheel away. Kneeling by Furness, he said, "Take heed of his words, my lord. You owe him your life this day."

Chapter Twenty-four

Low, pearl-gray clouds blanketed the sun. The comtesse and Joanne had marked minutes, then hours, before surrendering to sleep.

The little French butler did not know what to do when, ushering a bleary-eyed Dr. Ames into the morning room, he found the comtesse seated at the table, her head resting on her hands as she slept. Joanne was curled asleep in two chairs she had pulled together.

"I will wake them," Ames told him. "You may go—all is well."

With dragging steps he went to the chairs where Joanne lay. After gazing a long while, he went on to the table. Gently he laid his hand upon the comtesse's shoulder.

At the touch she sat upright. The question came to her eyes as soon as she realized it was Ames.

"Lord Jason is unharmed," he hastened to assure her in a whisper.

"And Lord Furness?"

"He is quite weak and will be convalescing for

some time but I believe him to be past danger. I would have come sooner but for tending him."

"What time is it?"

"About ten, I believe." He fumbled in his coat pocket. "Jason said to give this to you."

The comtesse reached for it slowly. "He is not coming?"

Shaking his head Ames said, "He has left London. I do not know where he has gone. Mayhap the letter will tell us."

"There was nothing for Joanne?"

The voices, though hushed, aroused Joanne. "Benjamin! Jason? Is he . . ."

"No, he was not injured."

She slumped back in relief, her heart soaring in thankfulness, her prayers answered. She jumped up joyfully and ran to hug the comtesse, but her aunt's look disquieted her. "Why has he not come with you?" she asked, turning back to Ames.

"He has left London," Benjamin answered gently.

"Why did he not come to me—at least to bid me farewell?" Her gaze went from Ames to the comtesse. "Does he truly believe I wish to wed Lord Humbolt?" Distress filled her features.

"Lord Jason is . . . perhaps confused." Ames searched for words of assurance to ease Joanne's anguish. "I don't think he knows what to believe just now. He will return."

"What of my father?" Pain filled her face.

"A serious wound, but not mortal. I believe he feels some remorse. He indicated he would trouble you no further. He is a haunted man—to be pitied."

"I . . . I think I may . . may come to understand

what ruled his behaviour," Joanne said slowly. "Hatred is such a . . . a destroyer. Mayhap some day I will understand fully—even be able to . . . to forgive him."

The comtesse put her arm about Joanne, her heart aching for the young woman. She noticed Ames rubbing his eyes. "Benjamin, you can explain further this eve. For now you should rest."

"I am exhausted," he admitted. "If you will excuse me I shall go and return later."

"Of course. Thank you for coming, Benjamin," the comtesse told him gratefully. "I will take care of her," she answered his questioning nod toward Joanne. "We shall be able to think more clearly after some proper rest. Till this eve."

Ames nodded and walked tiredly from the room.

Joanne watched him go wordlessly. Drained by the tensions of the night, fear for Jason and his apparent rejection, she felt her world crumble. He had taught her how to go on and she would, but now the pain of his loss was too fresh, too deep. A sob escaped and she turned to her aunt for consolation.

Ames paused in the corridor as heartbreaking sobs came from the drawing room. Shaking his head sadly, he left.

"Let us do as Dr. Ames suggests," the comtesse urged Joanne. "You cannot continue this way." Her words had no effect on the drawn, pale figure staring out the morning room's windows. "For my sake then, please? The season is nearing its end. The heat will soon make London unbearable. Let us go."

"As you wish," came the uninterested reply.

"I will make the arrangements then," Ames told the comtesse as they walked slowly away from Joanne. "Has she been like this ever since I left London?"

"Her condition has worsened steadily, I think. At first she went out, but it is a month now and for the past two weeks she has refused to move from this house. She eats nothing, sleeps little. I am quite concerned. Is there still no word from Lord Jason?"

"None. Several times before I left I tried to see his brother, the Duke, but he was never in. Now they say he has gone to his country estate and I've received no answer to the letters I've written. I cannot understand it," he concluded shaking his head. "Have you heard anything about Furness?"

"Only that he has gone to Furness House—for an extended stay, the gossips say. Wiltham has disappeared, probably with every *sou* Furness had given him." She shrugged. "Joanne has not spoken of either of them. She only asks each day if I have had some word from Lord Jason. It is very difficult." The comtesse shook her head sadly. "But, your idea is brilliant. The fresh air and activity should revive her spirits. The children, especially Ellen, should renew her interest in life. This self-pity must be broken."

"That is what I hope for," Ames said, glancing back toward the wan figure they discussed. "But I must go if I am to make all the arrangements for your journey before I myself depart."

"We shall see you soon then. I believe we can be ready in three days' time."

He looked as if to question the wisdom of such a hasty departure.

"It will not be thought odd, that we leave so suddenly," she assured him, "I have let it be known that Joanne is not well." She looked appraisingly at Ames. "Have you thought what will happen if Lord Jason returns to Kentoncombe while we are at Irwin?"

For the first time during his visit, the doctor smiled. "It is the only hope, is it not?"

The piping of children's voices rang into the second-floor window at Irwin Manor. From it the comtesse could see a group of boys kneeling in a circle, intent upon the marbles within it. Some older girls sat against an outer wall, their sewing lying in their laps as they visited. Younger children ran back and forth, inventing some imaginary journey. She turned from the scene to answer Joanne's call.

"I am here, *ma chère*."

"In Dr. Ames's library, Aunt? With all these books? You must be desperate, indeed," Joanne teased.

"That is unkind," her aunt laughed. "But what did you wish?" *How much Joanne has improved*—non, *matured,* she thought. A tempered gaiety had returned since coming to Irwin.

"Oh, I am taking Ellen for a walk. I think we shall go to the orchards and see if the apples are ready. The gardener said two days ago that they were almost ripe."

"Good eating—do not stay too long," the comtesse said as Joanne left.

"I almost forgot, Benjamin wishes to speak with you. He asked if you would come to his study," Joanne told the comtesse. "We won't be too long," she called back as she hurried down the corridor.

With slow steps the comtesse went to Ames's study.

It was an odd summons, she thought. Joanne is right, I am desperate for company. "Good afternoon," she greeted the physician as he rose upon her entrance.

"A good afternoon it is," Ames said, walking around his desk.

"You are unusually cheerful," she noted.

"But is there not much to rejoice in?" he teased.

"If you mean Joanne, of course there is. The weeks here have worked wonders. Ellen was the key—the child has given us a miracle."

"Love is what she has given," he replied.

"*Oui,*" sighed the comtesse. "If only Lord Jason would return, mayhap all would end happily and I could journey back to London." She arranged her skirts. "But, you have not told me what it is you wish."

"I have had word," Ames stated.

"Word?" the comtesse questioned. The doctor's smile encompassed his entire face. "Well, tell me what it is before you burst," she twittered.

"Jason is at Kentoncombe."

"At last," she clapped her hands.

"And is to call here at any time."

"Now?"

"Yes. I expect he will want to see Ellen—she became a favourite of his after you went to London."

"But she is with . . ."

"Exactly!"

"Will it be wise to throw them together so?" she pondered aloud.

"No harm can come from it."

"A shock for them both, though. But," she smiled and winked, "I agree."

There was a knock and Miss Hampsen opened the door. "Lord Kenton is dismounting, Doctor. I thought you would wish to greet him."

"Thank you," he nodded. Ames held out his hand to the comtesse.

"I shall see him later—my presence here would arouse his suspicions," she said.

Ames turned to go.

"Benjamin?"

"Yes?"

"Joanne has taken Ellen to the orchards—the apples are ripening."

"To perfection, let us hope," he quipped.

"Benjamin, how good to see you," Kenton greeted his friend.

"We had almost forsaken your return," Ames replied.

"It has been long—too long. I was at a hunting lodge on my brother's lands for much of the time. Before I came home I went to London but . . . but the comtesse's house was boarded for the summer. No one seemed to know where she had gone, only that Joanne was ill. I dared not ask too many questions." They had reached Ames's study and both men sat.

"Would you believe I even went to Bath searching for them, but there was no trace of them there." He leaned forward. "Good friend, tell me, do you know how they fare? Where they are?"

"Yes to both questions," Ames smiled. "I am most happy to tell you that the comtesse is in good health, albeit desiring more society. Joanne is much improved also."

"Much improved? Was she very ill?"

"Not physically. Your departure without seeing her took her spirit after all that had happened." He studied Kenton closely. "She loved you deeply."

"And I her." He laughed weakly. "You are surprised to hear that from me? With good reason, I suppose. At the hunting lodge there was little for me to do but think what a fool I had been. What I saw of myself, of my actions that night, was not pleasant." He straightened, bracing himself, and asked, "Has a date been set for her marriage to Humbolt?"

"She refused him."

"Refused, then I still . . ." He rose. "You must tell me where she is, at once," he demanded, his face joyous.

"It may not be wise for her to see you. Let me think on it. Why don't you go visit Ellen. I know she will be delighted to see you. When you return I shall give my answer." Ames refrained from smiling in view of Kenton's threatening frown. "I believe she is in the apple orchard."

"Benjamin . . ."

"Not now. Go on. Ellen has grown so you will hardly know her."

Slapping his gloves against his leg, Kenton turned angrily and strode from the study. The echo of his boots had faded when the comtesse rejoined Ames.

"But what if he does not go in search of the child?" she asked.

"He sought her company when Joanne left. He will do so now."

* * *

"There, that red one. No, to the left." Joanne tried to guide Ellen's hand as she held her aloft. "Good. Now taste it," she said, setting the child back to the earth. "Let us sit here—on the grass.

"Is it ripe?" she asked as Ellen's small mouth chomped obediently into the apple.

The little girl nodded eagerly, chewing the juicy hunk. She sat beside Joanne and offered the unbitten side.

"No, I shall get another in a while." Joanne looked about. The cheerful mien she carried when around others wilted away. "I walked here once with Lord Jason," she told Ellen confidentially. "He lectured me on the proper way to care for fruit trees. Of course I did not pay the least attention." Falling silent, she plucked aimlessly at the grass as she recalled that day. Other memories came; a single tear rolled to the edge of her cheek.

"Why do you cry?" a thin voice piped.

Startled, Joanne looked about—no one was there but Ellen.

"Why are you so sad when you speak of Lord Jason?" the same voice asked.

"Ellen," Joanne said, looking at the small child who sat staring up at her in wide-eyed seriousness. "Ellen, did you speak?" she asked in amazement.

The child ignored her question. "I don't understand. When Lord Jason speaks of you he is sad also. If you both love each other, why is that?"

"You can speak!" Joanne shouted and hugged the child to her. "You can speak," she said slowly, holding Ellen back to look at her. "And all this time we thought . . ." The child's words suddenly rang in her ears. "You said we both love each other—Lord Jason and I?"

Ellen nodded slowly.

"How do you know Lord Jason loves me?" Joanne asked, a tightness closing about her heart.

"After you went away, he came oft to see me and took me riding. I even got to hold Asteron's reins," Ellen beamed proudly.

"And?" Joanne prompted.

"And he would give me sweets and sometimes let me feed Asteron a ca—"

"No, no," Joanne interrupted. "What did Lord Jason say about me?"

"Why the same things you say about him. That he missed you and that he loved you." Ellen frowned at the other's thickheadedness.

"Ellen! Ellen, come to me!" a voice well known by both reached them.

Joanne gasped as she recognized it. Trembling she realized Jason had returned at last. She raised a hand to still her racing heart. She had prayed he would come, but now that he had she was filled with fear.

"Ellen! Ellen!" he called again.

"Go to him. Go on," Joanne urged, springing to her feet and pulling the little girl up with her. She watched Ellen run off joyously. Could she have been telling the truth? Did Jason love her? Then why had he waited so long to come?

Joanne wrung her hands and debated running away. *Do you love him?* an inner voice asked. *Oh, yes,* her heart cried out in answer, and her indecision was gone. *Fight for his love if you value it,* the voice continued. Yes, yes, she trembled with expectation. Ellen would bring him. Dear Ellen would bring him to her once again.

"Oh, my little miss." Kenton caught the little girl up as she ran to him and tossed her lightly in the air as he had oft done in days past. He hugged her gently. "My, how you have grown," he beamed at her as he put her on her feet and took her hand.

Ellen motioned for him to follow her.

"No, I must get back to Dr. Ames," he told her.

She tugged desperately on his hand, trying to lead him forward.

"What is it you wish to show me?" Kenton laughed. "I will come—lead the way." He released her hand. Following the little girl brought to mind another time she had led him and with that memory fresh in his mind, he beheld Joanne beneath the apple tree. His heart did a somersault. He drew a sharp breath. *My God,* he thought, *she is so lovely.*

"Aren't you happy to see her?" Ellen asked in her tiny voice.

Kenton's eyes moved from Joanne to the child looking up at him expectantly. His eyes widened in wonder. "Ellen?"

"Yes, she can speak," Joanne said, slowly walking up to the two. "She spoke just moments ago to me." Tousling Ellen's hair gently she added, "Is it not a wonderful miracle?"

Kenton picked the little girl up and kissed her cheek tenderly. "Very wonderful," he smiled at her. "You are a very special little one," he continued softly and hugged her tightly, gazing at Joanne.

"The apples are ready to eat," Ellen told him seriously, pushing back in his arms.

"Are they?" Kenton returned absentmindedly, drinking in Joanne's beauty, the gentle smile playing upon her lips.

"They are. And they taste good too. Do you not want one?" the child asked.

"No," he shook himself. "But I tell you what," he continued, returning his attention to her and setting her down. "I bet Dr. Ames would love to have one—this one." He turned to the tree behind him and picked a large red apple. "Could you take it to him for me?" he asked, putting it into her hands.

She shook her head eagerly.

"Good girl. Run now—tell him we shall come along soon."

They watched her scamper off.

Jason turned to Joanne, his pulse racing. He studied her features, trying to read her thoughts—to feel his way at how to best do this. "Has she been speaking long?" he asked, awkwardness descending upon him.

"No, the first time was just moments ago. It surprised me so." She searched his face for a sign—a sign that would tell him that what Ellen said was true. She longed to reach out—to feel his arms about her.

"How did it happen?" he asked softly, stepping nearer.

"We were sitting over there—just talking, rather I was talking and suddenly she wanted to know . . ." Joanne swallowed, the beating of her heart was deafening, surely he must hear it. Surely he must see the love she held for him ". . . wanted . . . asked why we were both sad when we spoke of each other. She said . . . we loved one another."

"Do you love me?" Kenton asked quietly, a grimness coming over him.

Joanne had but to raise her hand to touch him. All at once her fears returned. "Do not be cruel, my lord," she said turning away.

His hands caught her shoulders and forced her back to face him. "I could never be cruel to you again, my love. Say only that you forgive me . . . and . . ." he faltered and ended weakly, ". . . that you love me." His love, his desire blazed in his eyes, flowed into her being from the pulse in his hand holding hers.

"Oh, Jason." She could speak no more as joy overwhelmed her. The past two months' grief was forgotten as he crushed her to him, his lips demanding satisfaction.

Kenton drew back in wonder. "I thought I had lost you forever. It was worse than if you had died." He shook his head and caressed her cheek. "You are truly in my arms," he marveled. "After . . ."

Her fingers touched his lips. "Do not speak of it— say only that you love me." The longing in her eyes fanned his desire.

"I love you, my Joanne." He pulled her closer, bent to kiss her.

Joanne's hands stiffened against his chest, causing him to halt and gaze at her questioningly.

"Let us agree not to speak of the past," she said

earnestly, taking his hand and fingering the scar upon his thumb gently. "Let us agree to start our time together from this moment."

He nodded his understanding.

Her arms circled his neck as she yielded to him, drawing him close to her.

Sometime later Kenton reluctantly drew a deep breath and gazed fondly at Joanne, who was radiant with happiness. He sighed. "They will wonder if we do not come."

"Only Benjamin, perhaps," she returned. "The comtesse will need no explanation," Joanne continued with arched brows.

Giving her a playful squeeze, he noted, "I think I rescued you from the comtesse too late."

"Ah, but the education she has given me will benefit you," Joanne sallied.

"All my fears are confirmed," he laughed. Taking her face in his hands he breathed, "How I do love you." His kiss, a gentle pledge of love, became much more as she met his desire with her own.

At last it was Joanne who spoke, trembling from the flame he had aroused. "I fear we must return to Irwin. You must make a hurried journey."

"I must?" He cocked his head, amused.

"To London, for a . . . what do they call it? A special license. And do you think you could speak to a solicitor while you are there—about Ellen?" she asked, biting her lip, wondering if she dared to ask too much. "Could we not adopt her?" she spoke in answer to the question on his face.

"Not yet married and we have a child?" Jason

feigned shock, then kissed her fearful look away. "A most excellent idea," he assured her.

"On second thought, the comtesse and I will go to London with you," Joanne told him, straightening the folds of his stock. "The comtesse has been longing to return to society."

"And then we can make use of that special license much sooner." His voice deepened intimately as he drew her close. "I am to wed a wise woman."

"But what else could I be?" Joanne returned with arch innocence. "With the 'education' I was given."

"I am most anxious," Kenton said tenderly as he bent to kiss her, "to continue the education of Joanne."

Love—the way you want it!

Candlelight Romances